IMAGINE BREAKING EVERYTHING

Lina Munar Guevara

Translated from the Spanish by
Ellen Jones

PEIRENE

First published in Great Britain in 2025 by
Peirene Press Ltd
The Studio
10 Palace Yard Mews
Bath BA1 2NH
www.peirenepress.com

Originally published in Spanish as *Imagina que rompes todo*
in 2022 by Himpar editores, Bogotá, Colombia

ISBN 978-1-916806-12-2 / eISBN 978-1-916806-13-9

Cover artwork: María Berrío. *A Cloud's Roots*. 2018.
Collage with Japanese papers and watercolor paint on
canvas. 203.2 x 243.84 cm / 80 x 96 inches
© María Berrío. Courtesy the artist, Hauser & Wirth,
and Victoria Miro Photo: Jeannette May

Designed by Orlando Lloyd
Typeset by Tetragon, London
Printed and bound in the United Kingdom by TJ Books

The authorized representative in the EU for product safety and compliance is Easy Access System Europe – Mustamäe tee 50, 10621 Tallinn, Estonia, gpsr.requests@easproject.com

This work is published with support from the Reading Colombia programme, co-financing for translation and publication.

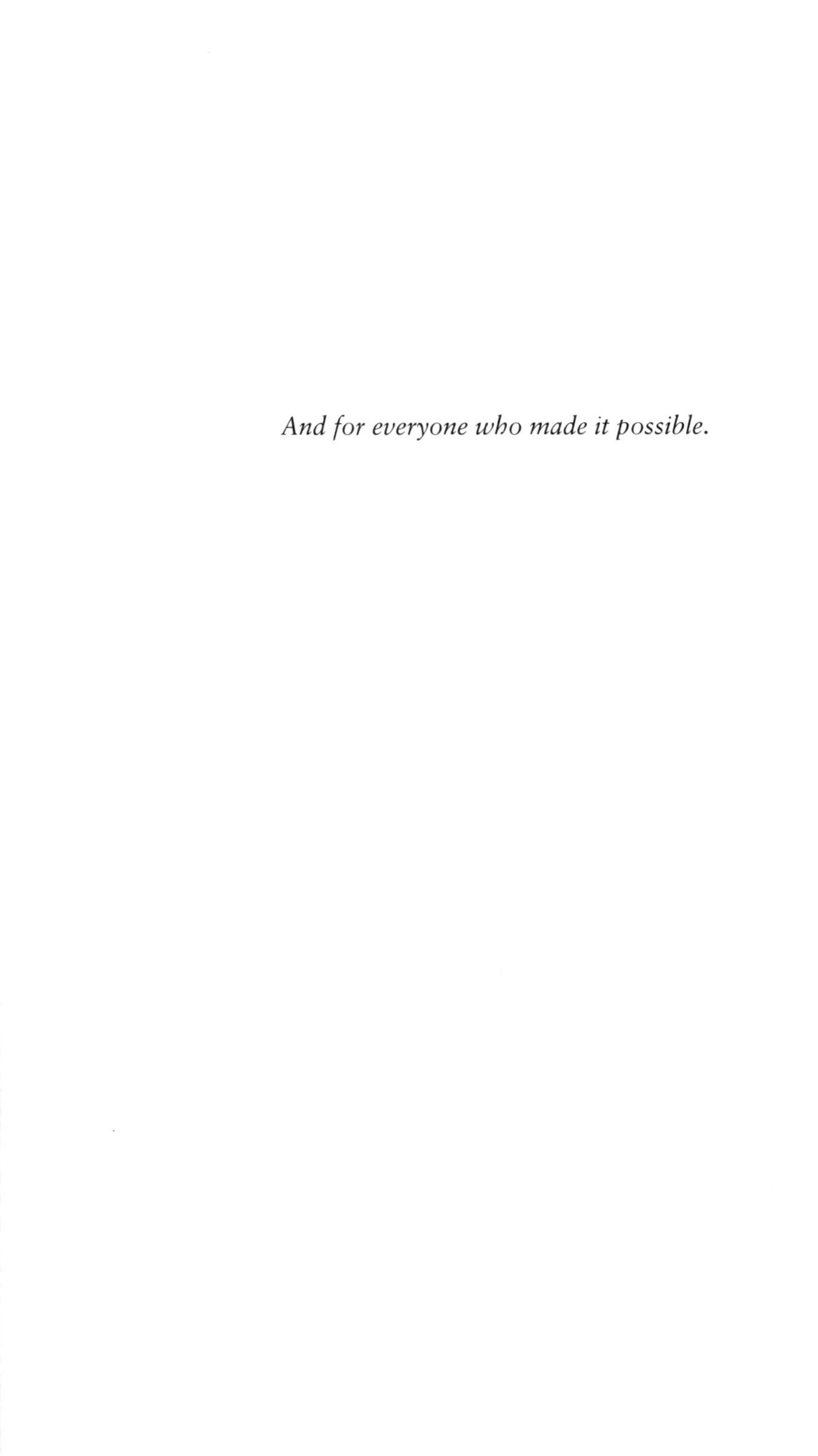

And for everyone who made it possible.

You've got to get out of this town, I always say
that's why I took the initiative, took cocaine
but according to my uncle, who is dead,
No matter where you go, you take it all with you.
I feel full of life but also
I can't bear it.
You've got to get out of this town, I still say,
though I've already left.

SILVINA GIAGANTI

'You Take It All With You', *Slow to Turn Off*

FRIDAY

‘So, what are you going to do?’

I just sat there. Stiff. Margarita, the admin woman, was looking at me. She was smiling, but her face still reminded me of the one the history teacher always wore. He’d ask a question then grab his marker pen, start tapping it on the desk, and say, ‘It’s not calculus, ladies, there’s a finite number of answers.’ ‘Answer me this, grandad,’ Zapata would murmur, with a hand gesture to go with it. She’d say it quietly so only I could hear. It would make me laugh, but also want to throw my rubber at her so she’d let me think. And the teacher would keep banging on about how it wasn’t calculus or whatever, his dumb way of saying, ‘It’s not that hard, Noriega, answer the fucking question.’ The question asked by Margarita, the admin woman, wasn’t calculus either. There wasn’t an infinite number of answers. In fact, there was only one, and unlike with the 1854 civil war, this time I knew how to reply.

‘Graduate.’

Margarita laughed softly and leaned back in her chair as if I had just told a joke.

‘I mean after that.’

I looked at her. Despite being relegated to the admin building and not hanging out with either the teachers or the students, Margarita had the same air about her, the same tone of voice. It felt different to my previous school. It was as if they, Margarita and everyone else, were all made of the same stuff, something I lacked and was incapable of learning. For her, and for everyone at the high school, graduating was no big deal. It wasn't a deal at all, in fact it was the natural course of things. Inevitable. But at my previous school, the Corpus Cristi District School, that wasn't the case. Nobody graduated. Graduating didn't figure in anyone's plans, because by that age, people had already started working or living with their boyfriends or had 'got into trouble'. Sometimes all of the above (like Mum). It was harder to find reasons to stay at school when help was needed at home. But I was going to graduate. That's what I told my aunt, Anahí, every time I handed her my report card. 'Not top of the class,' I'd warn her, 'but I'll graduate.' She nodded, but I was convinced she hadn't taken it in. That's why I was surprised the day she called me into her bedroom, where a handful of dresses was thrown over the chair in the corner. She asked what the other parents would be wearing to the graduation. 'How should I know,' I replied, but grinned like an idiot all the same. I didn't give a toss if Margarita the admin woman said I was going to graduate – she didn't know me – but if my aunt believed it, it might actually be true.

Still, I had my doubts. Five years after leaving Corpus Cristi, I remained scared of waking up back there. 'You can take a girl out of the barrio,' Mum's friend Adela warned her when we left, 'but you can't take the barrio out of the girl, baby.' It's true: you can recognize someone from Corpus Cristi as far off as Korea – they're the one who, when a car backfires, flings themselves to the ground with their hands over their head. I exaggerate, but only a little.

Margarita, the admin woman, opened my folder.

She must have been looking over my marks, checking those numbers that had cost me sweat, blood and tears; every mark out of ten I'd scraped together and that no longer meant anything. Just stains, no more important than a bit of coffee or lipstick on the page: once they'd stamped PASS on the report card, that's all they became. There it was, in blue ink, the tops of the P and the A slightly faded, but there all the same, and there was nothing the teachers could do about it; not the history teacher, not the calculus teacher, not the catechism teacher, none of them could change it. PASS, bitches. If they'd added things up wrong, if they'd failed to mark an absence, well, they were fucked, because I'd passed every single subject and was going to graduate. *Not top of the class, but I'll graduate.*

Then Margarita, the admin woman, made a face and I knew. I knew before she opened her mouth: the printer.

'I'm sorry, love,' she sighed, looking at me as though she'd just run over my dog. 'I can't give you the green light.'

It all went to shit with that cocksucking motherfucking printer.

The worst thing about this story, the thing we need to remember, is that I'd had the money to replace the printer. At some point in my life, I'd had it, and I turned it into a tattoo, some earrings, and an avocado-shaped coin purse. You absolute mug – who the fuck even uses a coin purse? I've never used a coin purse in my life, why would I start now? If I was going to spend the money, I should at least have spent it on something I'd use, something good. Anyway, the point is, I promised Margarita I'd pay her first thing on Monday morning.

'That'd be Tuesday, because we're not in on Monday.'

'Even better.'

'No, no, love. You're not listening,' she said with the same smile. 'It's not possible.'

'Please…'

'The thing is, love, today's the last day of the accounting period,' she said, and I nodded, serious, as though I understood the implications of a fucking accounting period.

I told her I'd bring it on Tuesday without fail, that I already had the money (not true), and could she please let me bring it because I needed to graduate, please, my mum was coming all the way from Bucaramanga just for my graduation (not true either, as far as I knew). She looked at me for a moment and I looked back. Margarita, the admin woman, had blonde hair with highlights in it, and square, blue-rimmed glasses that matched the button-up jacket she was wearing. I wondered if she had glasses in every colour and changed them each day depending on the jacket she was going to wear. She had coin purse written all over her, and I thought of offering her an avocado-shaped bribe. But no, people who look like they use a coin purse rarely turn out to be bribable.

'I have to graduate,' I said instead. 'Please, I'll bring the money on Tuesday.'

'I can't—'

'Tuesday without fail.'

'I just can't, darling. If I made an exception for you I'd have to do it for everyone.'

But no one else at this school needs an exception, do they, Margarita? Nobody else has this problem, nobody else is being hounded by a printer. Only me.

'I'm begging you. Please, after everything that's… I have to graduate, please.'

'I—'

'I've done everything, everything they asked of me, the lessons, the tests, the final exams, the community service, everything, I've done everything. It's not fair not to let me graduate because of something that's got nothing to do with, because of something that… because of a… an accident. Please. I'll bring the money on Tuesday. I swear.'

She sighed, defeated.

'First thing on Tuesday.'

I jumped up out of the seat with a smile. Then I remembered I didn't have the money.

It's fine, Melissa, this is why you have a job.

I went from school straight to Señor Héctor's shop. It was two blocks (which felt like three when it was raining) from Aunt Anahí's house, in barrio La Alborada. I was proud to spend two weekends a month in that little shop, organizing the shelves, cleaning the floor and the toilets. They rarely trusted me to cash up because the till never worked properly and maths wasn't my thing – infinite answers and all that. I liked mopping the corridors, because I could do it to songs by Sergio Vargas, who Señor Héctor loved, and it was nothing but back and forth, like painting a house. Or what I imagined painting a house would be like – I'd never actually painted one. Corpus Cristi was constantly under construction but hardly anyone ever bothered with a final paint job. Most houses remained a colour somewhere between earth and mustard yellow, with concrete columns, and the ones that were painted tended to gradually add on balconies and extra floors painted in different shades or with patches to cover up the graffiti. That was one thing the walls were good for. The whole neighbourhood was one giant canvas.

In La Alborada, on the other hand, graffiti never lasted long at all. Señor Héctor once made me clean the façade of the shop where a tag had been sprayed. It wasn't the first time I'd had to clean a piece of graffiti, but because this one wasn't mine, it took forever, and my wrist was sore by the time I was done. People usually left the shop alone, because Señor Héctor didn't mind selling stuff on credit, plus he'd installed those lights that come on by themselves when someone walks by. The idea of standing under those lights, can in hand, in full view of the world, was enough to discourage most people. Unlike in Corpus Cristi, in La Alborada appearances mattered. Señor Héctor got his fair share of tags even so, but the lights weren't a total waste because when people sat outside boozing I'd sometimes wait for the drunks to fall asleep before going past and triggering them to come on. They'd get such a fright they'd fall out of their chairs, which was a good laugh.

When I got there, the outdoor spotlights were off because it was still light out. Inside, merengue was playing and Señor

Héctor was arranging tins of tomato sauce. 'Tomato purée,' Aunt Anahí would correct me. I approached Señor Héctor with my head bowed, like when Katya creeps over with her tail between her legs after pissing on the carpet. And he must have realized I'd come to ask for an advance because he didn't even look at me before saying: 'There's no cash, Meli.'

That's what happens when you trust any old stranger to pay you back, Señor Héctor.

'Please, Don Héctor. I'll work the whole month, two months, however long you need, but I need some money super super urgently.'

He went over to the till. I followed him, biting a bit of cuticle off. Mum always used to tell me off for biting my nails, so instead I worried at my cuticles until I yanked them off. Héctor gave me twenty thousand pesos – not even a tenth of what I needed – and dumped a bag of prawns on me that were about to go off.

What the fuck am I supposed to do with a bag of prawns?

'Fry them up with garlic and olive oil,' Anahí said, inspecting the bag. 'We'll have to peel and de-vein them, but they're still good.'

'De-vein' was a nice way of saying we had to pull out the shit.

'The digestive tract,' she corrected me.

'Which is full of shit,' I insisted, leaning on the counter. I crossed my arms and sighed. 'Just some of it,' I begged her. 'Just a little bit, please. It would be a loan. I swear I'll pay you back every peso.'

'Get the spaghetti out, and some parsley from the fridge,' she said, opening the bag of prawns. 'Remember what I said when you broke the printer? Oh, and a lemon.'

'Yeah, I know, but I'm desperate. Please, I swear I'll pay. How much parsley? This much? I'll pay you back double, triple, if you want, even though that'd be usury, but of course you know more about that than I do.'

I loved teasing her for working in a bank, saying that bankers were a bad lot, the worst, and that (unlike Señor Héctor) they never trusted anyone.

'My my, aren't you the funny one. Put some water on to boil. I'm sorry, Meli, but I did warn you.'

I sighed loudly, so she would hear my sigh and know I was fed up.

'Slice the garlic nice and thin.'

'I'll pay you quadruple if you want.'

'It's not about the money, Meli. Every action...'

'Has consequences, yeah yeah, but Auuunnntie.'

'But nothing. Now watch, kid, this'll come in handy.'

'I doubt it, unless it's money,' I said through clenched teeth.

Still, I watched as she slid the knife along the prawn's flank (do prawns have flanks?) and, using the tip, pulled out the brown thread with a single tug. Anahí made cooking pretty. It was a pleasure to watch her. And her food was always delicious.

She looked lovely when she cooked, too, because she enjoyed it. She had an old-school glamour, sort of faded, like those black-and-white photographs of actresses. She gave the impression of being from a previous century, though she was barely forty. She had a pianist's hands. I didn't say so because I knew she didn't like her hands, long and thin, perfect for tossing a frying pan around like it was second nature. Yeah, they were a pianist's hands, though she hardly ever played anymore, and the keyboard in the study was mainly used as a desk, covered in notebooks, invoices and a dusty-leafed succulent. The story goes that my aunt used to play all kinds of things on that keyboard, from Beethoven to Flans, and of course Alejandro Sanz. Anahí loved Alejandro Sanz, and she also liked some of his songs. I bet her hands looked great when they were playing, especially when she painted her nails bright colours. They were a salmon colour right now, which was pretty, but I didn't tell her that either, because it was boring and I didn't want her to stop painting them the golds and blues and occasional greens that suited her so well. She'd dyed her hair a reddish brown that suited her too because she was all pale. I, on the other hand, can only ever have black hair because my skin is dark. Anahí has the same brown eyes as Aunt Magdalena, and I have my mum's honey-coloured ones. A shame, because my dad has green eyes. You'd think he could at least have given me those.

When the olive oil was hot, my aunt put the prawns on to fry. I wasn't sure whether I liked prawns. The only time I remembered having eaten them was at Aunt Magdalena's, during a novena, back when she still invited us over. It must have been a long time ago, when Mum and I still lived in Corpus Cristi, when Aunt Anahí was still Uncle Roberto. Aunt Magdalena served them in a glass bowl soaked in a kind of pink slurry, with slices of sausage and adorned with bits of lettuce. I remembered how the first one I tried made me want to throw up, but because I still liked Magdalena then, I made the effort to wash it down with a gulp of Coca-Cola. I bet she didn't de-vein them.

When I put the garlic in to fry, I suspected I was going to like these prawns. The smell wafted around the kitchen. Garlic is super important because it goes with everything, like onion, but, unless you're making something al ajillo, it shouldn't actually taste of garlic. You need just the right amount so that it's overshadowed by the other ingredients. Anahí explained this to me as she stirred the pot of pasta. My job was the parsley. She showed me this cool way of chopping it, see-sawing the knife quickly from side to side, like one of those guillotines they use in stationery shops, zip, zip, zip. I enjoyed that, moving the knife in one direction and then the other, feeling the little bits come off on the chopping board. It was a good way of clearing my head, like mopping or painting a house.

'Smaller,' she said, and took the knife off me to do it herself.

As she went on cooking, I crouched down to stroke Katya, who'd got up to stretch at the smell of the prawns in the pan. She was a caramel cocker spaniel with brown eyes and a few grey hairs on her nose. She yawned and stuck out her pink tongue before resting her head on my knees, as she did whenever she wanted me to stroke her neck. I obeyed, and she lay back further and further until she was belly-up on the tiles.

'Is that nice?' I asked her, patting her stomach, where she had these little whirlpools of fur. 'I'm going to sell Katya. How much do you think I'll get for her?'

'She's so naughty you'd have to pay someone to take her off you.'

Katya was my first pet. Well, she was Anahí's, but now that we'd lived together for five years in her flat in La Alborada, she was mine too, really. In Corpus Cristi I never had pets because a) Mum and I were never home, and b) I wasn't great with animals. Back then I wasn't great with people, either. 'You were no angel,' as Anahí put it, which was a nice way of saying I was a real piece of shit. I scratched Katya's belly till she started swiping her paw, while Anahí mixed the pasta with the prawns.

'Squeeze the lemon on,' she said, tipping some pasta water into the pan.

I pinched a bit of powdered soap and washed my hands thoroughly before grabbing the lemon. It was already sliced, so I squeezed one half against the edge of the pan. The juice ran through my fingers and made the little strips of raw flesh sting where I'd tugged at the cuticles. I ignored the pain and squeezed out a bit more. It had never occurred to me before to put lemon in pasta, but I'd learned that lemon is a bit like salt. It sort of fixes the flavour. Cooking is full of contradictions, like the one about putting salt in cake mixes. That's why it's so interesting. It's not like solving an equation, following a series of rules step by step until you get to X, boring old X that can never be anything other than itself, X. When you cook, you never know what you're going to end up with. Even if it doesn't look like it does in the book, even if it doesn't taste like it's supposed to, every dish is worth the effort because you can never make it twice, not really. See, cooking is like magic, transforming ingredients, making them disappear and reappear. If you end up with the same as what you started with, you haven't cooked, full stop. I wanted to have my own restaurant; I probably wouldn't cook there, but I'd spend hours watching the chef.

That's why I'd gone to register my interest in Business Administration. That was the answer Margarita the admin woman was looking for. I hadn't told anyone, that would have jinxed it. Well, hardly anyone, because Aunt Anahí knew, and I'd also told Santiago. I'd even told him the bit about the restaurant, but not the whole idea, because I was embarrassed, and embarrassed that I was embarrassed about it. I did tell Zapata, because I was never embarrassed about anything around her: she understood. I told her I wanted to have a restaurant that would be like an ordinary house or flat, where people (it had to be a small group) would come and leave their things in the dining room or living room. We'd give them a glass of wine and they'd go into the kitchen where they'd agree on a menu. Then the chef would tell each of them what to do and they'd help out with the cooking. The chef would give them easy jobs, of course, so they wouldn't ruin the dinner, but the trick was to make them believe they might ruin it if they did things badly. They'd eat the starter right there in the kitchen while the main course was cooking and then they'd sit in the dining room, and even though the food might not be as good as if the chef had done everything themselves, it'd taste even better to them. And after that they'd have dessert, which really was made by just the chef, because everyone else would be tired by then.

'But you have to open a bunch of restaurants first, Norieguis, to be able to finance it,' Zapata told me.

And I said, yes, that all I needed was one successful Italian restaurant and that would cover it. That's why I liked talking to her, because we understood each other. It's why she always played me her music, too. Zapata was a bit alternative. She was into a lot of weird music, some of it cool, some of it properly weird. When she played it to me, she'd always explain why the singer was doing X or Y, or who they'd been inspired by or why that album was the high or low point of their career.

Her music made me feel something, even the songs I didn't like. And when I did like them, my God, those ones went round and round my head for days, I couldn't stop listening to them. It happened with 'Running Up That Hill (A Deal with God)'. When I heard it, it made me feel like I was in this huge country house – rustic rather than elegant. We were having dinner at a heavy wooden table with candles because there was a blackout and I suddenly had to leave. When I left the house, it was daytime, though inside it had been night, and I ran up a dirt path lined with trees that had leaves like curtains. That was the drums, my footsteps through the fields of tall grass and twisted wire fences leading up to a green, green hill, not too high, but when I got up there I couldn't see anything but the blue sky, and that was where I spoke to God, not my grandad's God, everyone's God, and made a deal: that I would change places with someone I loved very much who had died, so that person could come back and I would go to heaven. I never knew who that person was. Sometimes it was me.

That's why the song sped up, for the trip back downhill, not too fast, just enough to let the slope do its thing. And I felt so calm and happy because I knew it was the sacrifice I'd made that allowed me to get back. I told Zapata this, that that's what the song had made me feel, and she said it was a lovely song, wearing a smile that seemed to say she'd hoped it would make me feel that way.

While Aunt Anahí served the pasta, I laid two places at the table. I checked the big chocolate pot sitting in the corner underneath the leak. The damp had got worse because the pot didn't usually fill up in just one day. I picked it up and emptied it into the kitchen sink before putting it back. There was a dark patch on the ceiling and the paint had cracked. Aunt Anahí came out of the kitchen with the food and Katya in tow, tail wagging. She put the plates on the table and collapsed into a chair.

I took a huge forkful of pasta and didn't care that it burned the roof of my mouth because it was delicious. The garlic had gone all golden so if you wanted to eat the little slices tucked among the spaghetti, you could. The prawns: *so good*, especially drenched in the olive oil. I told my aunt how good it was, and she said I needed to have faith in her recipes. Then I begged her again to help me with the money for the printer, but she wasn't budging. So as a sign of protest I decided to answer my phone. An unknown number had been calling me over and over.

'Hello?'

'Hello? Melissa?'

I felt a thrill go down my spine. I hadn't heard her voice since my birthday, seven months ago.

'Meli, are you there? Can you hear me?'

'Mum? You got a new number.'

'Yes,' she laughed. 'Oh, it's so nice to hear your voice, love.'

She said she was going to be in Bogotá at the weekend. I almost dropped the phone. Were my hands sweating?

'I'd love to see you,' she said. 'We could spend the weekend together.'

The weekend. The weekend together. The whole weekend together. I was so surprised that I only clocked that I hadn't said anything when she asked, worried: 'Have you got plans already?'

'What? No, of course not. I want to see you.'

'Then I'll come and pick you up tomorrow, darling.'

SATURDAY

One of my first memories of our flat in Corpus Cristi is of kneeling on the sofa, my hands and forehead pressed against the window. I was trying to check if the hopscotch I'd chalked on the pavement the day before was still there, but I couldn't quite see from the living room. The radio was on in the kitchen and because the flat was tiny you could hear Joe Arroyo singing wherever you went. It started to smell like burnt plastic and gas, so I knew Mum had turned the oven on. I ran to the kitchen barefoot, and Mum told me off because I might get spattered with hot oil or step on something. I ignored her, running over and asking what she was making.

A chocolate cake, from a box. We were going to take it to Aunt Magdalena's – she was organizing a piñata that day. Mum turned the box over and read the instructions out loud. I remember the yellow cardboard against her painted nails, their purple and black stripes. How old would she have been? I was about four, so Mum must have been about twenty.

'Want to help?' she asked.

I nodded and she lifted me up onto the counter. She touched my nose and told me to hold the plastic bowl while she poured in the instant mix. A cloud of brown powder rose up. The kitchen filled with the smell of chocolate. Mum turned up the radio and started dancing as she opened the drawer to get out the utensils. She's always been a good salsa dancer and, like with everyone who's good at salsa, it was obvious even when she wasn't dancing, even when she was doing something as simple as opening the oven door. I wanted to ask her about Dad, but didn't, maybe because it was a nice day and soon there would be chocolate cake.

My dad was a black hole that killed conversations. If you got too close, bam! he sucked out all the air. That hasn't changed. And it wasn't fair because, back then, I always wanted to talk about him. Not *to* him, never to him, just *about* him. Even much later, after he left, after he left for good, you could still feel him in the flat, like a kind of ghost, hiding in the most unexpected places. Sometimes he showed up in a dirty sock he'd left behind that had got mixed up with all the others. Sometimes he was the way Mum smelled when she came home at dawn, or the sound of one of his local friends laughing, or that feeling of wanting to cry – 'to mewl', as he'd put it. Sometimes he was silence itself, inside the flat. The silence that, back when he was around, Dad would use to give Mum a fright. Out of nowhere he'd sing out into the silence – not properly, just an off-key shriek or two, before falling quiet again as though nothing had happened. It still makes me laugh. Not just because of that voice he'd use, but because of Mum's reaction, too. He only ever did it when she was there. 'Ay, Andrés,' she'd scold him, slapping him on the arm as he laughed. That's why he did it, so she'd tell him off, to annoy her. It didn't have the cruelty he did everything else with, he was just fooling around. Sometimes, when the flat was silent, I would still expect to hear him singing. People say I've got a half-sibling somewhere in town. For all I know there's a whole bunch of them out there.

I could have asked Mum, but it was a nice day, and we were listening to salsa in the car. We were in a silver Chevrolet with Bogotá license plates. It was Adela's, Mum explained. We were going to hers for the weekend, she said. Outside, people were walking, shops were open, a taxi driver went by with his arm hanging out of the window, so close I thought it was going to get caught on our wing mirror. All completely normal, except none of it was normal, because Mum was there, sitting next to me, and we were going to spend the weekend together.

'I've missed Bogotá,' she said, 'the movement, the chaos.'

She looked different. She'd dyed her hair light brown and cut it short. Her eyes looked smaller because she wasn't wearing any eyeliner and she was dressed like the mums in those ketchup adverts: carefully ironed lilac blouse, white jacket slung around her shoulders and black trousers that weren't baggy but weren't tight-fitting either. The only thing that was the same was her nose, bent slightly to the left and with the same pink mark where she'd once had a piercing.

'Even the traffic jams?' I asked her, smiling.

Even me? Did you miss me? Do I look different to you? I hoped so, I hoped that just by looking at me she could tell how much I'd changed.

'God no,' she laughed. 'I haven't missed the traffic jams one bit. But tell me about you, love... How's school?'

'I'm still on the basketball team, but we've had a shit season.'

I realized I'd said 'shit' and glanced at Mum to see if that was something that annoyed her these days. I couldn't tell, but figured best not say it again just in case.

'I'm sure next season will be better.'

'This was the last one, I'm about to graduate.'

'Graduating already! When did that happen?'

'No idea.'

'What about your boyfriend?' she asked, with a complicit smile.

'We broke up last month.'

'Oh no,' she said, before taking my hand and linking her fingers through mine.

She used to do this whenever Dad was giving us grief. Not when he got aggressive, then she'd send me to my room, but when he started raising his voice. Mum would take my hand like that, silently, as though to say, 'It's nothing, forget about it.' And I'd look at her and she'd smile at me, wrinkling her nose, and I'd think, *It's nothing*. I liked the gesture so much I didn't want to tell her that I wasn't sad about having broken up with Santiago, that I'd been sick of him anyway.

'Was he the one I met?' she asked. 'Kind of skinny, glasses…'

'Alex? Ah no, no, this was another guy.'

She was, like, two boyfriends behind, but I didn't think this was worth pointing out.

'There'll be better ones to come. How's your aunt? I'd have liked to come up, even if just to say hello.'

I'd told her Anahí had gone out early to run some errands, but this was a lie. The truth was we'd had a fight. When I told her I was going away with Mum, she said she didn't think it was a good idea. Defiant, I asked why not. And she started on about Mum just turning up with no warning, how it wasn't fair, not a word from her all this time then out of the blue she shows up, etc., etc. What pissed me off was that my aunt thought she knew more than I did about my relationship with Mum. She always thought she was an expert in everything, even this.

My aunt and I hadn't spoken that morning (only a brief 'see ya') but I wasn't worried. I knew it was only a little fight, nothing compared with the ones we used to have when I first moved into her flat in La Alborada. No, this was nothing like that. Those were proper fights, Fights with a capital F. The worst ones started after Mum moved out, when my aunt and I had to learn how to put up with one another. Well, mainly she had to learn how to put up with me (I mean, let's be fair).

I used to want to break everything. I'd shout at her, slam the door in her face, call her 'Roberto' and other things I'd rather forget. One day I grabbed a ceramic Japanese cat from the living room and flung it against the wall. It smashed. I hadn't meant to break it. I don't know what I was expecting to happen, but when I heard it break it was like I suddenly snapped out of it. I was about to pick up the pieces when I heard my aunt's footsteps coming down the corridor. I ran out of the flat. I spent the rest of the day outside, even thought about never going back, about getting on a bus to Bucaramanga to look for Mum or even just going round and round the block forever. I abandoned the idea as soon as it started getting dark. It's easy to be all brave and everything while the sun's shining, but at night – that's something else. At night the city transforms. Facing Anahí's fury seemed like nothing next to staying out in the streets by myself or ending up sleeping at Social Services. I rang her doorbell knowing that as soon as it opened she'd scream at me, call me all kinds of names, even tell me to turn right around and never come back. I was ready for that, but the sneaky cow just took one look at me and gave me a hug.

She hugged me and I just stood there uncomfortably, caught off guard. She told me to sit down in the living room and then warned me that the cat statue had been the last ugly thing in that flat. This was debatable (my aunt had questionable taste), but I wasn't going to say so just then.

'What I mean is,' she went on, 'you can't break any more of my stuff. Next time – look at me – next time, you're going to breathe, in, out, then count to at least seven.'

'Why seven?' I ventured quietly.

'I'll bet you can't even get to four without getting distracted. And if that doesn't work, you're going to imagine breaking things, but you won't actually do it, you hear me? You're going to imagine breaking the paintings and the table and the lamp and the curtains until you calm down. And if that still doesn't work, well, then you'll try again.'

The worst part was that I thought the cat statue was kind of cool (questionable taste runs in the family) and I was sorry it couldn't be fixed. However, breathing, counting and imagining I was destroying things actually worked – the more details I imagined the better. It took me a few weeks, though, before I could bring myself to ask something that had been bothering me ever since.

'Why didn't you yell at me?'

'Did you want me to?' she asked, laughing. When she saw I was still waiting for an answer, she added: 'Oh kid, people have been insulting me since long before you were born. I've realized it's hardly ever me that's the problem.'

'My aunt's fine,' I told Mum in the car. 'Kinda tired, but fine.'

There was a pause. I didn't like those silences. They felt like opportunities for questions nobody wanted to ask or answer. Questions that all boiled down to just one: are you all right without me? The question scared me because I didn't know how to say yes without her thinking I didn't still miss her. Even more scary was the answer she might give me. Neither of us asked. I thought about mentioning the money for the printer and asking if she could maybe help me out, but I couldn't bring myself to do it. I looked out of the window and asked if Adela still lived in Corpus Cristi. She said she did.

Going back to our old neighbourhood made me think of the time I went clubbing with Zapata and the other girls, and some time around two in the morning (when they start playing old-school music) this song by Tito el Bambino came on that I hadn't heard for ages. As soon as it started, I realized I still knew the words. It struck me as odd that I hadn't forgotten them, I'd just forgotten I knew them. Singing along happily was like finding a bit of me that I'd lost. Going back to Corpus Cristi felt the same, but without the happiness, because the bit of me I'd lost there was a piece of shit.

Everything looked familiar, even the few things that were new. Everywhere I looked, houses that were just concrete and iron skeletons, shops with plastic baskets full of mangos and avocados, the butchers with their red signs – everything just as I'd left it. Except I was completely different. Yeah, I was a different person… but I was scared of forgetting that. I was scared that when I got out of the car and set foot in the neighbourhood (even just one foot) it would swallow me up completely and spit out the old Melissa. I didn't smoke, but this would have been a good moment to start.

My relationship with cigarettes was – how shall I put it? – complicated. I should have liked them, but I hated them. When Mum, Anahí and I all lived together, when Mum and I had only just left Corpus Cristi, the flat in La Alborada was one big cloud of smoke. It was gross, or gross for me, at least, because the other two didn't even realize. Mum and Anahí smoked like they'd been brought up by the Marlboro Man, so I'd know that smell anywhere – I was like an airport sniffer dog. It was their gift to me, that ability. Which is why, one evening when I'd stayed late for basketball practice, I recognized the smell before I even went into the toilets by the school gym.

Nobody smoked at Ofelia Uribe Secondary. It was clear those in charge at my new school took the no-smoking rule seriously (they took all rules seriously). Whoever was in the toilets knew this too, which is why they'd waited till classes were over before lighting up. Now, I didn't want to get into any trouble, because things had been going surprisingly well for me. At home, Anahí and I had finally found our rhythm, and at school – well, I still hadn't really got to know any of the other girls, but I didn't have beef with anyone or a problem with any of the teachers or anything. I didn't want to kick the hornets' nest. So I was tempted to get out of there, and I would have, except I was on my period and needed to change my tampon. I pushed the door, no doubt in my mind that someone in there was smoking.

Zapata almost fell off the ledge when I went in. She was sitting on the corner beside an open window, though it did little to dissipate the smoke.

'God, Melissa, you scared me,' she said, sighing. 'I thought you were Aguilar.'

Aguilar was our basketball coach. God only knows why he'd be going into the girls' toilets.

'No wonder you don't run,' I said, waving the smoke away with one hand.

It was obviously a joke, but Zapata didn't respond. She didn't even glance at me. Without putting down her cigarette, she went back to staring out of the window. I shut the door.

'You not training today?'

She shrugged.

I took my little washbag into a cubicle. If it had been anyone else but Zapata, I would have let the conversation die there. But during my first week, before everyone realized PE was the only thing I was good at, Zapata had picked me first for her team. It was like, I don't know, a vote of confidence, and I felt like I owed her.

'If you don't want to train today, I can tell Aguilar you're sick,' I said from the cubicle.

She didn't reply. When I came out, she had her head back and her eyes closed. I watched her chest rise and fall, a little shakily, as she tried to take slow breaths, the cigarette forgotten. I recognized the scene: she was trying to calm herself down, maybe trying not to cry.

'Mind you don't burn yourself.' I pointed to the cigarette in her hand. There wasn't really any risk of her burning herself, I just said it because I didn't know how to ask if she was OK.

She opened her eyes, as though she'd forgotten for a second that she wasn't alone, and took a long drag on the cigarette as she stared at the wall in front of her.

'It's just so… it's so…'

She took another drag and let the smoke stream out through her nose like a bull. I glanced at her, unsure what to say, as I rinsed my hands. I kept rinsing them even though all the soap was gone, because I didn't want to leave her alone in there. *Maybe she wants to be alone, you idiot.* Maybe she did, so I turned off the tap. Zapata stubbed out what was left of her cigarette in the wet sink.

'What time is it?' she asked me.

'I don't have a watch, but it's got to be four thirty by now.'

That meant practice had already started. She got down from the counter and cupped her hands under the tap. She swilled out her mouth and spat.

'Do I smell?' she asked, shaking her ponytail.

'Like you smoked the whole pack.'

'Fuckssake!' she shouted, turning off the tap. 'It's just... fuck... it's not fair. This was the only thing I had left. This shit was the only thing left where I... didn't have to think. And now even this is fucked!'

She kicked the bin, which wobbled a bit.

'I can't take it anymore. All I can hear is their screaming, even when I'm not at home. They never stop, it never stops. Even at school, I can't think, and this, this was the only thing... I'm an idiot.' She took a deep breath. 'Sorry, I'm done, I didn't mean...'

'I know.'

'What?'

'Not that you're an idiot. I mean, I know... I used to do anything to avoid going home, to distract myself.'

She looked at me. I sat on the counter. I think that was the first time I felt like Ofelia Uribe wasn't so different from Corpus Cristi District School after all. Or it was, but that rage Zapata was feeling, and that I knew so well, was a kind of bridge between the two. I didn't enjoy seeing her like that, but I was glad to know neither of us was alone.

'Want to go for a walk?' I asked her.

'Aren't you going to practice?'

'I've got period cramps,' I lied.

'Sure?'

'Shall I tell Aguilar you're not coming either? I can say you're taking me to the nurse, so he doesn't mark you absent.'

She looked at me for a moment before nodding. She gave a little smile and said:

'Thanks, Noriega.'

'Whatever you do, don't leave the cigarette butt there or we'll both be fucked.'

After that, I didn't see her smoking at school again. But I did at parties. If I needed to find her, like I did at Gómez's party, all I had to do was follow the smell. That party was torture, but I had only myself to blame, really. I should have left after breaking up with Santiago, but someone else was supposed to take me home so I was trapped until they wanted to leave or I could find another lift. Outside, the air was freezing and the wet grass was ruining my heels, which, to top it all off, were sinking into the mud. Never break up with someone in heels. And definitely never stay behind afterwards. I searched among the smokers in the garden and found Zapata leaning against the wall of the house, talking to someone.

'I broke up with Santiago,' I announced.

The other person looked at me, let out a 'yeesh' and left.

'All OK?' Zapata asked, not moving.

'He seemed chill about it. I guess he knew it was coming.'

'No, I mean are you OK.'

'Me? I would have broken up with him last week if I could.'

I'd postponed it because his dog was due to have surgery, not only for Santiago's sake, but also for Toto's – he didn't deserve the drama.

'It was past its sell-by date,' I said.

'I guess we knew it was coming, Norieguis. Two months and you're always: see ya, wouldn't wanna be ya. Why is that?'

'I don't need you playing the shrink.'

'No, no,' she said, shaking her head. 'I just mean, damn.'

'I'm not crazy.'

'I am,' she replied and paused to exhale cigarette smoke from her nose, 'but it's not obligatory.'

I looked at her in silence.

'Want some?'

I accepted the cigarette and took a drag. That was the thing. Everything pointed to me liking cigarettes. Because of my mum, my aunt, Zapata, I was very clear on the attractions of smoking, the moments when it was useful. But for some reason (because of my dad), I didn't like it. No, I didn't just not like it, I couldn't stand it. I only had to taste that semi-bitterness and I needed to stop, spit, and put down the cigarette, because it transported me immediately, without fail, to the staircase in our building in Corpus Cristi.

The steps were narrow, and I used to play parachutes there. I'd tie plastic bags to pencils to float them down to the ground floor. I wasn't playing parachutes that time, though – I was lighting a cigarette. I'd had it hidden in my pocket since the day before, but I had to wait till I could get hold of a lighter before I could smoke it. I remember flicking the little wheel until my finger was red but all I got were sparks. When I finally got the flame to stay lit, I brought the cigarette to my mouth and immediately started coughing. The cigarette went out, but the smoke and the cough remained. I was trying to get a flame again when I heard the footsteps. I was on the ground floor so all my dad had to do was open the door of the building and we were face to face. *Run, bitch.* I dropped the lighter and fled upstairs, two at a time, hearing his footsteps behind me. He was yelling God knows what. I leapt up the steps, feeling like my heart was in my throat and was about to choke me. Finally, the inevitable. He caught me by the shoulder, swiped the cigarette from my hand and grabbed my wrist so hard I could feel it throbbing.

'Where did you get it?' he shouted, not looking at me as he dragged me up the stairs. 'Your mum?'

'No!' I lied, but it was pointless. He shouldn't have bothered asking. Where else would I have got it?

He kicked at the door until Mum opened up. She looked at me. I was shaking. My wrist was throbbing so much it felt like my whole hand would swell up and burst like a water balloon.

'You'll never guess what the girl's been up to this time,' he shouted, dragging me inside.

'The girl', always 'the girl'. Sometimes he gave the impression he didn't actually know my name. Mum smiled at me, but I could tell she was scared.

'Go to your room, love.'

I'd got Mum in trouble. I looked at her, wishing I was brave enough to ignore her, to stay there and fight side by side with her, because if we were going down, we might as well go down together. But I couldn't do it. I ran and shut the door. To try and drown out what was coming from the other side, I scraped my knuckles against the wall, scraped until they stung, until the pins and needles went all the way up my hand and arm and drowned out everything else. They say the body can only feel one type of pain at a time.

I don't know if that's true, but what I do know is that, if I concentrated, I could make the whole world disappear with my knuckles.

When I gave her back the cigarette, Zapata thought the tears in my eyes were because of Santiago. She slipped her arm through mine and said: 'Let's go for a walk.'

Adela was the same as ever. New haircut, same Adela. She even smelled like the same perfume, one that got right up your nostrils and into your brain whenever she hugged you. Her flat was new, though. I mean, it was old, but Adela had just moved there; she used to live in a big old house with a courtyard and everything. Her new place was much smaller, on the second floor of a three-storey building. The stairs were wide – they would have been good for playing parachutes – and the flat was really bright. It had light-blue walls, a window with white curtains and a mini palm tree in a pot. It was similar to the one we'd had, but much more nicely decorated. Maybe because we always let the plants die and no one ever bothered to hang anything on the walls. We sat down to talk on the sofa in the living room.

'When did you refurbish, Adelita?' Mum asked.

'Six months ago, now.'

'What happened to the old house?' I asked.

Mum gave me a serious look, frowning slightly, as though I shouldn't have asked. Adela let out a long sigh.

'Legal issues, babe, they had to sell it quickly.'

'Ah…'

'It was for the best, the maintenance costs were insane.'

'Course,' I said. 'I'll miss the fig tree though.'

'That fig tree,' Mum said. 'How many times did you fall out of that bloody tree, Meli?'

'She spent more time on the ground than in the tree,' Adela laughed, before looking at Mum. 'After she almost cracked her head open, I thought you'd never let me babysit her again.'

'Good job I've got a thick skull,' I said, rapping my forehead with my knuckles.

'Yeah, thick skull and strong fists,' Adela laughed. 'When little Meli saw red, ooof, Holy Mother of God! I'll never forget how you left that poor kid, what was he called? The one from next door. Or that girl, the fat girl…'

I just nodded, saying nothing. I wanted to change the subject. I didn't want to talk about that, any of it, the things the old Melissa had done. I wanted to tell her I didn't get mad anymore – well, I did, but I didn't punch or kick anyone. *Just printers, right Melissa?*

I didn't know how to change the subject and it was Mum, who was also looking uncomfortable, who asked Adela how much it had cost to remodel the flat. While she was talking, I looked out of the window as though still looking for my hopscotch chalked on the pavement. For a moment I could see myself playing in the street with Karen and Dayana, my neighbourhood friends, jumping into puddles and playing ding-dong-dash.

Adela made arroz con pollo and chips for lunch. Mum and I helped her lay the table while the chips finished frying. The sizzle of oil and the smell coming from the kitchen reminded me I hadn't had any breakfast that morning. There's nothing worse than running out of the house in a fury on an empty stomach – except, perhaps, staying at home in a fury on an empty stomach. Thankfully, lunch was shaping up to be pretty good.

I could tell Adela and Mum were still as close as ever, because when we offered to help, instead of saying 'No, no, you sit down', Adela pointed out where the glasses and cutlery were. While I got out the forks, I wondered if the two of them had seen each other more than I'd seen Mum in the last year. Maybe Adela had gone to see her in Bucaramanga. Better not think about that. When we sat down to eat, Adela told us she was still working in the same old beauty salon, except she now did home visits for mani-pedis.

'What's that like?' Mum asked.

'It pays better, but with what I spend on petrol it works out practically the same. It's so expensive these days, I'm not actually any better off.'

'Just more tired,' I said, pouring everyone a fizzy drink.

'Super tired,' Adela replied, smiling. I passed round the glasses.

'What about you?' Adela asked Mum.

'I'm still in Mira Plaza,' Mum said before taking a sip of her drink. 'But if all goes well, I think I'm gonna come back to Bogotá.'

Adela looked at her in surprise. This was new information for me too, but I didn't react because I didn't want to let on to Adela. Mum said no more about the subject. Not even when she'd be back or what needed to go well for her to be able to come. I didn't ask either, pretending these were things I already knew, things she'd told me. I think

Mum did the same thing when I said I'd applied to study business admin.

Adela was the one who asked me all the questions. She wanted to know everything, university, school, my graduation, when, where, the ceremony, the party, especially the party. I wanted to be able to get excited knowing that I was going to graduate, but all I could do was give short, simple answers, and she kept asking on and on. I forced a smile and started to pick at my cuticle. Mum was silent. Silent and smiling and nodding as though she already knew all this. Why wasn't she asking anything? She didn't even seem excited about the idea. She didn't know there was a spanner in the works that might stop me graduating, she should have been smiling and asking what the other mums were going to wear. Nope, just silent. I pulled on my cuticle and ground my teeth. I felt a stab in my stomach. I couldn't handle Adela's questions anymore, or Mum's silence. I wanted them to swap places, for Mum to do the asking and Adela to listen. No. I wanted to know I was going to graduate. I wanted to be able to tell Mum, to invite her to the graduation, tell her a date and a time instead of giving vague, clumsy answers. Why didn't Mum ask? Did she know I wasn't going to graduate? That it was better to have no expectations?

I imagined what the plant pot would look like broken, the earth spilling everywhere, the little palm tree's roots exposed, the black mess on the carpet.

I stood up. Enough. I said I'd arranged to call my friends who lived locally, I wanted to see them. I thanked Adela for lunch and said I'd be back later. Before leaving the flat,

I was relieved to see the plant pot intact, the earth in its place. Outside, I sat on the steps to take a few breaths, in, out, letting the old Melissa dissolve in the air streaming out of my nostrils.

SATURDAY AFTERNOON

Karen was slow. Whenever we played ding-dong-dash, Dayana and I would sprint off (like you're supposed to) and she always got left way behind. Poor Karen, always left alone to face the furious neighbours. I used to tell Dayana it was what she needed – it was 'for her own good', as Aunt Anahí would say. 'This way she'll learn to be quicker,' I'd tell Dayana when, from our hiding place, we'd hear shouts as the neighbours gave Karen an earful. Little Karen never got cross with us. She always followed our lead, even letting us go up onto the roof of her house after we convinced her to let us chuck down balloons full of (watered-down) ketchup and mayonnaise.

We got very creative with groceries. Raw eggs in the locks on the doors at school, ají chile in Dayana's stepdad's toothpaste, mayonnaise in the hand cream – or was it the other way round? I can't remember. We probably did both.

I walked around town uncertain whether to call them. I really did want to see them, but I felt nervous every time I looked at their names on the screen. You shouldn't spend too long looking at your phone in Corpus Cristi, because the pavements are super uneven and there are holes full of rainwater where there used to be flagstones. One misstep and splosh!

That hadn't changed. Nothing had changed, everything was exactly the way I'd left it. The same cracked and crooked streets, bordered by the same patches of tall grass where I was told not to play as a little girl because there might be rats (the same ones, or their children, are probably still there today). I don't know why I felt nervous about calling my friends, when I genuinely wanted to see them. It had been so long since I was in touch. When we said goodbye, I promised we'd keep talking, that we'd be friends forever. 'Forever-ever?' 'Forever-ever.'

I called Karen. The phone rang a couple of times, and I hung up. *They haven't called me either this whole time.* But I felt like I was the one who should have made the effort. They were the ones who'd been trapped in Corpus Cristi, not me. I called Dayana, but it was engaged. Before I gave up and put my phone away, it began to ring: Karen, returning my call. I hesitated before answering, but only for a second.

'Um... hello? Karen?'

'Melissa?'

'Yeah, yeah, um...'

'Meli! Wow, it's been...'

Too long. Too long since we... She said she was fine, fine thanks. Her mum? 'Working, as usual.' And mine? 'She moved to Bucaramanga, a while ago now.' And to what did she owe the pleasure?

'I'm in town.'

'In Corpus Cristi?'

'Yeah. I wondered if… maybe… you wanted to grab a beer or something.'

'Course! Today?'

'Whenever you can, I'm here all weekend.'

'Today's good, give me half an hour to sort some stuff out, then I'm all yours. Remember Doña Flor's bakery?'

'Course.'

'Meet you there.'

'Let's tell Dayana too, I've been trying to call her.'

'I mean, we could, but I don't think she'll come,' she laughed. 'Dayis moved to Cali, like, a year ago.'

'Cali? How come?'

'Her stepdad got a job there. They all went.'

Once again, we'd left little Karen behind by herself. I felt like apologizing before hanging up, but instead I said I was glad I'd get to see her. As soon as the call ended, I put my phone away. Another reason not to look at your phone too much in Corpus Cristi is that somebody might nick it, especially as it gets later in the day. Not a good idea to be out late in this town. One time, the three of us saw these drunk guys get into a fight. I mean, we saw drunk guys fighting all the time, but this time it was serious. At first it was the same as always, a few punches, some shouting; one guy had a bloody nose and the other grabbed the front of his shirt. To get him to let go, the guy with the bloody nose grabbed a glass bottle off the pavement. It wasn't even empty. When he smashed it into the guy holding his shirt, beer sprayed all over the place. The other guy let him go, but he kept hitting him with the bottle and the glass didn't break like it does in films. He beat him with the bottom of it, one, two, three, four times, all in the face, until the guy's eyes were bleeding pinkish blood, because he was crying, and then he went down. Two other guys showed up out of nowhere to help the guy with the bottle and started kicking the guy on the ground. They even kicked his face, which looked less like a face than a shapeless treacly mess by this point, red and black, dissolving onto the pavement. 'Let's go,' Karen said, tugging at my sleeve. She was crying too. Dayana looked at me as though for permission, but I was rooted to the ground. I knew I'd have nightmares, but I wanted to keep watching. I'd never seen anything like it; it seemed important, something we ought to witness, to learn from. We left when the police arrived and one of the guys started shoving an officer, who was carrying a gun. The next day people said shots were fired but nobody died.

It was never a good thing when the police showed up in our neighbourhood. If they were all carrying truncheons, you knew they'd come to evict someone. It happened to Juana Rincón's family. Me, Karen and Dayana went over to her street after we saw a huge truck, a bunch of pickups with tailgates and, like, fifteen police officers. Men wearing suits and ties were giving instructions to these other guys coming out with furniture to load into the truck, and black bin bags with trouser legs or dolls' hands poking out. There were also men coming out with cats in carriers and birds flapping about desperately, bashing against the metal bars.

'Why don't they do something?' Dayana asked.

She was looking at Juana and her family, standing motionless beside the door to their house while the men dumped all their stuff in the street.

'Like what, exactly?' Karen asked.

'I don't know,' Dayana replied, 'something.'

I noticed that Juana was crying. It made me angry. *As if that's gonna fix anything.* Dayana was right, they had to do something, put up a fight, start shouting, something, and if they weren't going to do anything, the least they could do was endure it with dignity. Someone had to punish Juana for crying like that, but who was going to do that when her dad was crying right there next to her?

'Juana's dad's a queer,' I said. 'That's why they're being thrown out of the house.'

I repeated this at school, several times. By the time Juana was back in classes, everyone knew what had happened and why. They swallowed the whole story. I don't know why people always believed me. Nobody doubted it, though some people did ask: 'What's a queer?'

It was something my dad used to say; he said it a lot, especially when he was talking about Uncle Roberto. I knew it was bad, but I had no idea why or what it was exactly. I made sure I used the word all the time, so Dad wouldn't suspect I actually liked Uncle Roberto. I liked him a lot, even though I wasn't supposed to. How could I not, when every time he visited he'd bring me lollypops or coloured erasers or glow in the dark stickers? Fancy stuff. Plus, while the men in Corpus Cristi wore dirty old clothes smeared with grease and smelled like sweat or beer, Uncle Roberto always wore clean clothes, had neat hair and smelled like cologne. Double fancy. I knew, even then, that he was always looking out for Mum and me. I also knew that, despite all that, I wasn't supposed to like Uncle Roberto, because he was a queer. When people asked me what it meant at school, instead of replying, I mocked them for not knowing, insinuating that anyone who didn't know was probably one themselves. They stopped asking.

I could fool Dayana, but I think Karen realized I didn't know even half the things I pretended to know. She probably did know those things. I always got the sense that Karen played the fool so she could hang out with Dayana and me, because she was without doubt the cleverest of us three. She wasn't the best in class, not even close, but she was bright and actually did her homework sometimes, and whenever she did, she'd always let Dayana and me copy her. We always got caught, of course, because we all made the same mistakes. Karen was really good at geography, drawing maps and learning capital cities, that kind of thing. She made up this song with all the countries in South America and that's how we got through Social Science in Year Five. Besides, her mum was super clever – she'd even studied at the Universidad Libre.

On the way to see Karen, it occurred to me she might be studying at the Libre too, or about to start. Now that Dayana and I had left town, I figured she was finally able to study properly, that she'd probably done really well at school and would do well at university, too. *I wonder what you're studying, Karencita?* Something sciencey? Some kind of history? Something with numbers? Who knew, maybe even medicine, though I hoped not, it sounded like too many sacrifices for too little money. I could imagine her doing a thousand different degrees, but Karen probably couldn't imagine that I, yes, me, Melissa Noriega, the most stupid, the most useless, the most *me*, had also applied to university. That would surprise her, but she'd be pleased because it would mean we could talk for a while about how hard it was to choose an outfit for the interviews or how confusing the forms were or how nervous we were, waiting for a decision. Things that, as kids, I never imagined we would talk about.

I couldn't find Doña Flor's bakery because it no longer existed. Instead, there was now a massive Ara supermarket. Karen had neglected to mention that, but I knew I was in the right place. Doña Flor's bakery had been right next to the vacant lot with the cow, which was still there (though the cow was not), maybe waiting for someone to turn it into a supermarket car park.

It was me who'd seen the cow first, that night. It was dark, the only light coming from a lamp post on the corner. Something was moving behind the fence and when I got closer I saw her caramel head poke out to munch on some grass. 'There's a cow in there!' I said to Karen and Dayana, pointing, but neither of them believed me. I grabbed Karen's wrist and forcibly dragged her over to the vacant lot. Halfway there she shook me off violently because the cow moved and she got a fright. She went back for Dayana and told her to come over. Meanwhile, I went and touched the cow's forehead, but that spooked her and she moved away from the fence.

'She looks like Porky Pili,' I said, and they laughed. 'But skinnier. She's too skinny, poor thing.'

'Do you think they're fattening her up for slaughter?' Dayana asked.

'No, she looks like a dairy cow,' Karen said.

'You look like a dairy cow,' I said to Karen, with a gentle shove.

'Pretty sure you'd only get powdered milk out of those udders,' Dayana went on. 'She's gonna die for sure.'

'Then we should let her out,' I said.

'Oh yeah? And buy her a bus ticket?' Dayana replied, and Karen laughed.

We went to see her a bunch of times. We'd pick grass we found growing nearby and leave it inside the vacant lot. It wasn't much, but we did it for a couple of weeks until one day she wasn't there. Maybe she died or was just moved on, who knows. 'Maybe they took her to a farm,' Karen suggested. I laughed scornfully and told her to stop being so naive, the cow had probably died of hunger, but the truth is I was really sad she was no longer there, and I liked to think that, yeah, she'd been taken to a farm far away and that she was healthy and happy and fat.

The vacant lot looked smaller than I remembered it. It had a new fence, a metal one with thick concrete posts, crowned with spiral barbed wire. It looked elegant compared to the wood-and-wire fence from before. I leaned against one of the concrete posts to wait, taking out my phone to check for messages from Karen. I texted her to say I was here, then looked at her photos on Facebook.

She'd got really pretty. She'd always been pretty, but she'd had her eyebrows done – they'd been super thick before – and her eyes looked enormous. I searched for the last photo of the three of us together. God, it was awful. Those photos should be deleted, all evidence of our teenage years removed. I had a radioactive orange streak in my hair where I'd tried to bleach it with hydrogen peroxide, Dayana had multicoloured braces, and Karen was sweating. The photo was from my last day at Corpus Cristi District School. I was wearing a white shirt with marker pen all over it (I'd made everyone sign it). Who knows where that shirt ended up; I promised myself I'd look for it when I got back to Anahí's flat.

I was still looking at my phone when I heard the voices. Thick, deep men's voices. I couldn't hear what they were saying, but when I looked up I realized two guys were running towards me. *I'm about to be mugged.* Before I could move, one of them got to me and shoved me against the fence. It was my bad luck that I slammed into the concrete post instead of the metal sheeting.

I tasted blood, my knees shook and everything started spinning. I clutched my phone tightly. I feared a fist was on its way so I raised my free hand to protect myself, but I was so shaky and dizzy that I couldn't get it up in front of my face. The guys were talking quickly, I couldn't understand what they were saying. Then they ran off. I watched them go, not understanding why they hadn't taken my phone.

I leaned on the fence, trying to keep my balance. I put my phone in my pocket. Maybe it had been personal. I felt warm blood slip over my lips but didn't know if it was coming from my nose or my mouth. It had to have been personal, why else? My face was tingling from forehead to chin, and within seconds that tingling became a fierce burning. I was owed a punch by more than one person in this town. It was my nose, definitely.

They've broken it, I thought, *they've broken my fucking nose*. But no. I knew what a fracture felt like and this pain didn't even come close. I thought they might have sprained it though. The guys had been tall, but younger than me, they couldn't have been more than fifteen. They'd looked familiar and unfamiliar at the same time. Had we grown up together round here? Maybe they'd been kids when I left. I considered the possibilities and arrived at the most likely suspects: the Martínez brothers. It had to be the Martínez brothers.

Why did they have to go for my nose? The one thing I actually like. I'd have to check whether it was sprained. They'd definitely stained my top, which I liked even more than my nose. I ran my tongue over my teeth and pinched my nose carefully, leaning forwards like our basketball coach told us the time Zapata got elbowed in the face during a game. 'Head forwards, girls, never back.' I stayed like that for a while until I felt the need to spit. Thick red saliva settled on the pavement.

I was still dazed when Karen finally appeared. When she reached my side and asked worriedly what had happened, the first thing I said, even before 'hello', was: 'You're pregnant?'

'What happened, Meli? Are you all right? What happened?'

'Fucking Martínez brothers,' I said with a smile, but only a small one, so my face didn't hurt too much.

'Are you OK? Do you want to… I dunno, go to hospital?'

'No! Hospital? Come on, it's nothing. Be honest though,' I said, turning my face to the side. 'Does my nose look wonky? Is my modelling career over?'

'I don't know how to say this, Meli: I think it was already over.'

I looked at her, she looked at me, and suddenly we were laughing like we were still at primary school. She looked like she did in her Facebook photos, the recent ones, none of which showed that belly of hers.

'Jokes, you look gorgeous,' she said, and we hugged, finally. I held my chin right up so I wouldn't stain her jacket. 'Though I'd rather have seen you without so much blood.'

'Yeah, me too. Let's go and get some empanadas,' I said, seeing as we couldn't go for beers, 'and you can tell me everything.'

'You can tell *me* everything, you mean,' she replied, hooking her arm through mine. 'It's been ages since I heard from you.'

We worked it out: it was five years since we'd seen each other. She passed me a tissue so I could finish cleaning myself up and we walked half a block to a little empanada place where there were two empty tables, a jukebox with coloured lights and several posters of women on motorbikes wearing underwear – the most comfortable way to ride. When I smelled the fat and reheated oil, I knew the empanadas would be good, even though I'd never eaten there before. Karen had, because when we went in the woman at the till greeted her by name. We sat down at one of the tables.

There was a long, heavy silence. I had a thousand things to ask her, but I didn't know where to start. I didn't want to say the wrong thing. It felt like a first date. The empanadas arrived in a red basket with limes and ají chile. I took one, blowing on it.

'Are you still with your boyfriend?' I asked, trying to remember his name.

'Yeah, three years now.'

'Three years! That's ages…'

'Yeah…'

'But you're happy.'

'Yeah, I am, very.' She laughed a bit. 'He's lovely, you'll have to meet him. I'm crazy about him.'

I nodded. I bit off the end of the empanada, which was still hot. I fiddled with a plastic spoon for a bit while it cooled down, dipping it into the ají before realizing it was probably better not to have any chile because it would only irritate my poor nose. I wanted to ask, 'You're pregnant?' again, but she hadn't answered me the first time, so maybe she didn't want to talk about it. But we couldn't not talk about it, right? It was right there, and it was important, very important. I couldn't pretend not to see her belly.

'So,' I said finally. 'You're…?'

'Yeah, yeah…'

'How far along?'

'Six months.'

'Six months, wow, congratulations.'

Congratulations? Congratulations wasn't what I wanted to say, not even close, but it felt like what you're supposed to say. What the fuck, why do we have to feel so different? If this was the old us, sitting here, I wouldn't feel like I had to say anything I didn't want to.

'How did your mum react?' I asked her.

'She's happy.'

'Yeah?'

She nodded. No, that couldn't be true, or rather, it couldn't be that simple. Karen's mum was one of the cleverest people in town and she always – always, ever since we were little – wanted Karen to go to university, to travel, to do things nobody in Corpus Cristi ever did.

'What about you?' I asked. 'Happy?'

'Yeah, I am.'

Silence again. We each ate our empanada, maybe so we wouldn't have to talk. It hurt to chew and I could taste blood, so I put mine down and tugged at a bit of cuticle on my index finger until it came off.

'Shall we get a drink?' she asked.

'Yeah, good idea.'

She got up and walked to the fridge. Her belly wiggled. I looked away. Every time I saw it, I felt like I was seeing Karen naked, because I couldn't shake the feeling that she wouldn't have told me if she hadn't had to. If she could have taken off her belly and put it away in a drawer before coming, she would have. I was no longer someone she shared that kind of thing with. Still, she'd decided to come and see me. Yes, she had decided to come and see me, knowing I'd take one look at her and know. I smiled. Maybe I also owed Karen that: the truth.

'Honestly, I'm a bit surprised.'

'Imagine how surprised I was.'

I laughed, taking one of the cans she'd brought over.

'So… what are you thinking? I mean… what… what will you do?'

'For now, Jaime and I will both live at my mum's place.'

'Does he work?'

'Yeah, in a carpenter's workshop.'

'And you?'

'No, I know nothing about carpentry.'

That made me laugh and I gave her a little slap on the arm.

'Seriously, though.'

'I'm working in a restaurant.'

'Ah...'

'What?'

'Nothing, I just thought, maybe you'd enrolled at community college or at the Libre like your mum.'

'No, yeah, that's the idea, but afterwards. Right now, we need to save money and I'll need more free time. I'd like to though, when Luciana's older.'

'You've already chosen a name?'

She nodded.

There was a pause so that I could say that Luciana was a lovely name, but that wasn't what I wanted to say. I owed Karen the truth because we'd known each other a long time, because we'd learned to add and subtract together, to do our make-up and use tampons, because I'd stayed over at hers all the nights I didn't want to stay at mine, because we weren't strangers, because there was still time for Karen to do things differently.

'But...'

As soon as I started talking, I knew I should stop. I remembered that look Mum had worn, the one that said: 'Don't ask that.' Too late.

'Did you think... have you thought... if you really want...'

'What?'

Her smile disappeared. It sounded less like a question than an accusation.

'Yeah, you know? If you really want...'

That, that moment right there, would have been a good time to stop. To pretend I never said anything, to eat my empanada. To leave it alone. But I'd started and I had to go on, not for me but for her, because I knew how this story ended.

'If you really want it.'

She looked at me, saying nothing. I went on.

'I mean, I don't know... there are agencies... there are places... you don't have to raise it yourself... her, raise her.'

'Of course I don't *have* to, but I love her.'

'I'm sure you do, it's just, it's not...'

'Not what?'

'It's not... not a good idea.'

'What the hell do you know about it, Melissa!'

'What do I know?'

'Go on, tell me. You always think you know everything, right? But what do you know about it, Melissa? You don't know anything.'

'I lived this, Karen. You don't have to shout at me. How old do you think my mum was?'

'No, Melissa. This is completely different. You can't compare...'

'Course I can, it's the same shit, and I can't believe you, you of all people, could have been so...'

'So what?'

'Well, so stupid!'

'It's always the same with you, isn't it? You know everything, right? You always, *always*, think you know more than other people, telling everyone what to do or not do, but we're not twelve anymore, you don't know anything about anything, and if I cared about your opinion I would have asked for it. Just because your life is shit doesn't mean it's got to be the same for the rest of us.'

I imagined getting up, leaving, throwing the empanada in her face, but I didn't. I breathed and counted and breathed and then I saw her, and the words dissolved in my mouth. I really saw her. This wasn't a stranger, this was Karen. Karen, wearing the same face as when she had to stand up in front of the whole classroom and her voice started shaking and her hands had to fiddle with something. And I was worried about her, like I always worried when she started her presentation and went all red but then had to start over again because the teacher interrupted her with 'Louder.' I didn't want to leave, I didn't want to shout at her. I wanted to hug her because it wasn't rage making her lip tremble, it was fear.

Right then I realized that what Anahí used to say was true. The problem wasn't me. I mean, it was, because I'd obviously touched a nerve and (to top it off) said she was stupid, but that wasn't the problem. Karen was scared. I breathed out hard, like I'd just done ten laps in PE and could barely stand up straight.

'You're right,' I said. 'It's none of my business, I'm sorry.'

She nodded slowly, hesitantly. I looked at her and nodded too, to make her realize I wasn't going to say anything else, that I wasn't going to argue. Besides, it was true: what did I know? Maybe Karen would study next year, maybe she'd be really happy, maybe she'd make it all work. After all, if anyone could, it was her.

'I'm sorry,' she replied, looking down. 'I didn't mean what I said. I'm a bit all over the place recently. Really, I'm sorry, Meli.'

I wanted to ask her if she really thought that – that my life was shit. In the end I decided not to. What was she going to say?

'It's OK,' I concluded.

Her shoulders started to relax. She looked at me, then at my uneaten empanada.

'No good?'

'Just tastes like blood.'

'What happened exactly?'

'The Martínez brothers, I think? Pretty sure it was them. I remember them as little kids.'

'Yeah, those two turned into a couple of bums, for sure.'

'It was probably about the cat.'

'Hey! You won't believe who I saw the other day… Pilar!'

'Villareal?'

She nodded.

'I didn't know she still lived round here.'

'Yeah, yeah, she's still around, she still lives up by the football pitch with the cross, she just changed schools.'

Pilar. Pilar Villareal. Hearing her name out loud made my body feel heavy, too real, too long and lanky for the plastic chair I was sitting on. I tried to shift into a comfier position, moving from one side to the other, but it only made it worse, I just ended up more uncomfortable. I'd tried for so long to not think about her that it caught me off guard, hearing her name like that. It was like Karen had just described one of my nightmares, revealing that it hadn't been a dream after all, it had all been real.

'We were so awful to her,' Karen said.

She said 'we' out of solidarity. Yes, we'd all called her Porky Pili, sung it at her and made jokes, but it was me who was the real dickhead. It was me who stuck drawing pins into her 'to see if she'll deflate'. Me who complained loud enough for everyone to hear when we were put in the same group. Me who shoved her into puddles. Me who oinked and snorted in the corridors and at break and in PE and when she was walking home. Me who spat in her lunch 'so she'll stop gorging herself for once'. It was obvious she'd left school because of me. And to top it all off, I ended up leaving too, only about four months later, though at least that wasn't on purpose.

'I saw Víctor the other day, too,' Karen added.

I don't know if she'd noticed my distress, but I was glad she changed the subject.

'Víctor!' I smiled at the thought of him. 'How is he?'

'Same as ever. He graduated last year and he's working with his dad.'

'Is he still hot?'

'He put on some weight after he hurt his knee and couldn't play football anymore… but he'll still do.'

We laughed, and she went on.

'You know that after you left, he told everyone you were his first time?'

My cheeks started burning and my hands sweating. Was it too late to swallow a spoonful of ají and blame it on the chile? Instead, I picked up my drink and took a long slurp to cover my nervous laughter.

'Melissa! Melissa Noriega! You and Víctor? Really?'

'At my leaving party.'

'At...? Like... during?'

I covered my eyes and nodded, laughing.

'Melissa!'

Víctor said it would be my leaving present to him. God, he was dim sometimes – the leaving present is for the person who's leaving. Thank God he was pretty, because he really was stupid. Though I wasn't much better.

Karen was still quiet.

'What?' I asked. 'I never told you?'

I knew I'd never told her, because I'd never told anyone. I was embarrassed. Not because of Víctor, I did like him, stupid and all. It was because I was sure I was the first girl in our year group to lose her virginity and, even though I was leaving, that was important. So important, in fact, that at Ofelia Uribe I made up that my first time was much later, with another boyfriend. What an idiot. It was probably like our periods: we all thought we were the first to get it when really we all got them at pretty much the same time. Or, who knows, maybe I really was the first to have sex. In any case, it didn't seem important anymore.

'I can't believe it, Melissa,' Karen said. 'You know how many people I told to go to hell because I thought they were spreading rumours about you?'

'They probably still deserved it.'

We started talking about people from our year, who was going out with who, who had cheated on who, who had left, who was still the same. It was strange to think Karen and I shared that world, that she knew a side of me no one at Ofelia Uribe knew, not even Zapata, because even if I told Zapata about my first time with Víctor it would be no more than a name to her, a year, an age, a curious titbit. She couldn't put a face to Víctor's name, the old Víctor, or to the old me. Even if I told Zapata everything, she'd never understand like Karen did.

It was the same with the whole time I lived in Corpus Cristi, which after all was a lot longer than I'd been in La Alborada. That whole part of my life belonged to those who were there with me. Karen knew me in a way Zapata couldn't, in a way Zapata never could, and yet it would have never occurred to me to talk to Karen about my idea for the restaurant or about the song that made me feel like I was on a hill talking to God. Karen was thinking about jobs and names and caesareans and cots and marriage. It was like she'd suddenly grown up and left me behind. If I talked to her about restaurants or songs it would be like when a child runs over to show their mum a drawing and all she can do is stroke their head and say, 'How lovely,' barely looking at what's on the piece of paper. I felt a bit sad about that. I would have liked to tell her those things.

Karen paid. I tried to because I'd been the one to invite her out, but she was faster. I said thank you and when we were on our way out, I asked: 'Hey, what do you think happened to the cow?'

'The cow?'

'Yeah, the cow from the vacant lot. Cafecita, the one we used to feed grass, remember? The cow from the lot.'

'Oh, yeah,' she said, but she didn't sound convinced. 'What happened to it again?'

'We never found out, one day she was just gone.'

'Maybe she was sold to a farm.'

I liked that she gave the same reply she'd given when we were kids, even if she didn't remember the lot or the cow. I gave her a long hug goodbye. Karen was busy the rest of the weekend so we probably wouldn't see each other again before I left. We promised to be in touch more often. 'Don't be a stranger.' 'Right back atcha.' When I passed the cow's lot, I thought that if I had to choose between knowing and not knowing what had happened to her, I preferred not knowing, because that way, who was to say that she hadn't been taken to a farm, that she wasn't doing well, that she wasn't very fat and very happy indeed.

SATURDAY NIGHT

When I was little, I thought if you had a heart attack your heart exploded like a bomb, and your chest would be drenched in red on the inside. I imagined that's pretty much what my nose looked like after the punch from the Martínez brothers. From the outside it looked a bit swollen, and still throbbed, but who knows what it was like on the inside. All kinds of fucked up, probably. At least it wasn't crooked. They say dying of a heart attack doesn't hurt that much, but maybe that's just so you don't think the person suffered (or only a bit). No way of knowing.

When Grandad Rafael died and we went to sort out his flat, Mum found a photo of him holding me. I don't know how old I was, less than one. You could just see this really round head with a patch of hair, wrapped in a blanket. Grandad was wearing a white jumper with a yellow zigzag on the chest, his messy black hair and several-days-old beard streaked with grey. He didn't look like a grandfather, he must have been about forty-five at the time. He looked like Aunt Anahí when she was still Uncle Roberto: same cheeks, same lips.

Grandad Rafael looked tired, like he'd been out running – like his granddaughter had kept him up all night, crying. Tired, but happy. When I saw the photograph, I thought of the afternoons I spent visiting Grandad and Uncle Roberto in that flat. I was Grandad's favourite, so he let me eat whatever I wanted and always had a bag of chocolates or sweets ready for me. Grandad couldn't eat that kind of thing. 'My blood's sweet enough already, darling,' he'd say, scolding Uncle Roberto whenever he helped himself to a treat. 'Leave something for the girl,' he'd growl, but Uncle Roberto would make off with it anyway, holding my gaze and a finger to his lips as though to ask me to keep the secret. Even though it was already dark by the time he got home from university, he'd always play with me for a while before sitting down at the table to study. He'd leave the TV on for me, on one of the kids' channels – they were the worst, boring as hell, but I watched them because it was him who had put them on for me.

I was Uncle Roberto's favourite too, maybe because I was his first niece. I beat my cousin Juanchi to it by two months. It wasn't much, two months, but it felt like a lot. Those two months meant my cousins had to do anything I said. I was also a lot more fun than Juanchi, who was always thinking ahead to the telling-off we were going to get. I don't blame him, I might have turned out as boring as him if I'd had Aunt Magdalena as my mum, but since I didn't, every time I saw my cousins I'd push them to the limit. Don't be such a chicken, let's jump, and they'd jump; let's swing from our hands, and they'd swing; let's scare the neighbours, and they'd scare the neighbours.

At Grandad's wake I dared them to steal a flower from the wake being held in the room next door. None of them managed it. There was more movement in the room next door than there was in Grandad's. There were a bunch of people in there, men and women going in and out constantly, wearing military uniform. Grandad had been in the army, that's why his wake was held there, but there was hardly anyone in his room because all his fellow soldiers, who would otherwise be coming in and out in their uniforms, were already dead.

I kept myself entertained with my cousins. We didn't have long to try the flower thing because a few minutes after we went into the hallway between the two rooms, Aunt Magdalena and Aunt Anahí came out too. I thought they'd tell us off for being outside or because, somehow, they knew what we were trying to do, or – and this was a constant fear of mine – for not crying. Because you were supposed to cry at wakes – girls were supposed to, anyway – but I wasn't. I didn't like crying; I hated it. In any case, the telling-off never came – neither of my aunts even noticed we were there.

Aunt Magdalena was shouting at Aunt Anahí (as usual). I don't know if this time she was furious because Anahí had worn a dress or because she wanted to read during the mass or both. Anahí was red in the face, not shouting or insulting her, just quietly repeating: 'He was my dad too, Magdalena.'

Uncle Roberto becoming Aunt Anahí and my grandad's death both happened in the same year. I know Anahí told my grandad, but I never found out how he responded. I can't imagine what he might have said, either. If Grandad knew my uncle had boyfriends, he never mentioned it, not even when everyone else was saying things like, 'Maybe this year little Roberto will finally get married for us.' After the change, Grandad wouldn't have been able to feign ignorance anymore, he'd have had to say something. I don't think he'd have said anything bad, I can't imagine Grandad being unkind to anyone. That's why I can't picture him in the army, either, but he was, and who knows what he did while he was there, how many people he hurt. So I don't know what he said to Aunt Anahí. Maybe he didn't even understand what she was telling him.

The day of the wake, when they argued, Aunt Magdalena left in tears. Anahí stood in the hallway, rubbing her forehead and pinching her nose as though someone had elbowed her during a basketball game, as though Magdalena had broken her heart and the blood in her chest was about to spill out of her nose. And I didn't know how to fix it. I didn't know anything about how to fix things, I only knew how to break them. So I just stood there watching her. Her cheeks were red and her eyes, which were filling with tears, looked lighter, but she didn't cry. When she realized I was watching her, she gestured to me to follow her. I thought maybe she'd tell me to stop spying, but she just said:

'Let's go and get a coffee.'

I leaned my head on her arm as we walked. I could sense people looking at us as we went past. Soldiers in their dress uniforms, men in suits, women in black dresses, eyes, eyes, eyes. Eyes that made my cheeks burn. Anahí must feel them too, right? Still, she walked on like it was nothing. No, not like it was nothing. Like she was too tired to worry about people staring.

The woman in the café gave us a particularly nasty look. For a moment I thought that she wasn't going to accept the note Anahí was trying to pay with, but after a while she took it reluctantly, as though touching it might make her break out in hives.

'Bitch,' I complained, loud enough for her to hear me.

Aunt Anahí said nothing. I wanted her to laugh or even tell me off, to say anything at all. We sat down. The coffee was boiling but she took one quick sip after another. I didn't know what to say to her. Don't listen to Aunt Magdalena? Sorry about Grandad? That I loved her? Why bother when she knew these things already? I rested my head carefully on her shoulder.

'Who…' I eventually asked, 'who taught you how to walk in high heels?'

'A friend, a long time ago.'

'I thought it might have been my mum.'

She smiled, a small smile, but a smile nonetheless.

'Come on, kid, who do you think taught her?'

'Really?'

She nodded and took another sip of coffee. I wondered if back then Aunt Anahí had known she was a she, if she'd always known or had figured it out at some point later. I couldn't bring myself to ask, so instead I said: 'Will you teach me?'

'Any time. Though you'll never have to wear heels.'

'Why not?'

'You're going to be super tall.'

'Shut up.'

'I'm serious.'

'I'm the shortest in my class.'

'Exactly, that's always the way, you'll shoot up, just wait and see.'

I wouldn't have believed anybody else, but Anahí had such a unique way of saying things. When she talked about what was going to happen, there was never any doubt in her voice. It was like she could pop to the future like someone popping round the corner, so you had no choice but to believe her when she talked about what was there. That's why I used to be glad we ended up at Aunt Anahí's whenever Mum and I fled the house at midnight. She always seemed to have the answers.

It's funny, though. Anahí has always lived in the same flat, but it feels like two completely different places to me, like at some point it split in two. My room, for example, is nothing like the guest room where me and Mum curled up together to sleep, despite it being the same room, the same bed, even. They only look alike on nights when I toss and turn and lie there with my eyes open, staring at the ceiling. On nights like those, they seem so similar I almost expect to hear Mum and Anahí murmuring together in the dining room.

That was what it was like the night Dad shoved me against the wall. He'd never done that before, not to me. I don't even remember what it was for. The girl must have done something, the girl had always done something. It was the first time, but it didn't feel that different from usual. It didn't feel like a big thing. It didn't feel like a thing at all, just the natural course of events. I fell on my arm and, more than pain, I remember this fierce heat, and not being able to get up. I heard Dad say something, but he was talking very fast and I couldn't understand what he was saying. He wasn't shouting, it was like he couldn't breathe. I felt like I ought to say sorry. Mum got up and we headed for the door while he was still talking.

We were in a taxi. I couldn't remember getting in. It was like a dream, only I knew I wasn't asleep because my whole arm was tingling. When we got to Aunt Anahí's, which was still Uncle Roberto's, she'd got my room ready, which was still the guest room. That night, Mum and I slept in the same bed. I should say 'sleep' in inverted commas, really, because Mum and Anahí stayed up talking for ages outside. I was in bed, lights off, under the covers, exactly as Mum had tucked me in, stroking Katya, who had come to lie on the bed. 'Relax, try and get some sleep,' Mum had said quietly before giving me a kiss on the forehead. But how the hell was I supposed to sleep? My arm was killing me, she was outside crying, the phone was ringing off the hook, my stomach felt like it wanted to come up out of my mouth. I'd rather have stayed in the dining room with the two of them. I'd rather have watched TV with the volume up high or taken Katya for a walk. I'd rather have had Dad not push me. I don't know how long it was before they turned off the lights outside and Mum came into the room, trying not to make any noise because I had my eyes closed so she'd think I was asleep. She got under the covers and I snuggled up to her. When she put her arm round my waist and I felt her breathing, for a moment life was the same again, like it had all been a dream.

I woke up with a nasty bruise. It looked like a painting of hate: big black brushstrokes, red, green, yellow, like the screen savers on the computers at school if you don't touch them for a while. Mum and Anahí argued about whether to take me to hospital or not. If they did, Mum said, there was a chance Social Services would take me away. Better not, she said, unless it gets worse.

I said it didn't hurt, even though it did, because I felt like there was a pact between Mum, Dad and me: if we all did our bit, we could go back to normal. Not feeling pain, that was my part. Dad's part was being sorry, that's why he came over to Anahí's every day. Mum's part was to forgive him, when the time was right – she had to wait just long enough to punish him but not so long that he lost interest, that way it would be the three of us again and things could go back to the way they were. For some reason none of us wondered why we were making such an effort to go back to normal when normal was so shit.

I'd got blood on my top. I'd tried everything to get it off, but it was no use. When I got back to Adela's flat I'd have to pretend it was a bit of tomato or ají chile or whatever, anything but blood, because I didn't want Mum to suspect it hadn't been an accident. If she realized, I'd have to invent some excuse, anything so she wouldn't find out the Martínez brothers had shoved me up against a fence. If Mum found out, she'd ask why, and if she asked why, I'd have to invent something so as not to tell her that, when we were still neighbours, I used to make fun of the Martínez brothers' speech (they alwayth talked like thith), that I used to yank their damp clothes off the line, that I'd stolen their lunch on more than one occasion and, above all, that I'd killed their cat. And if I made something up, she'd realize, because I wasn't very good at lying anymore (I was out of practice).

I didn't mean to. Kill the cat, I mean. I thought it would be funny to put laxatives in the food bowl the brothers left outside the door to their house. It *was* funny. I'd done it a couple of times before and, apart from the mess, there was no lasting damage. Then one day the fucking cat up and dies on me. Never trust a cat, not even to stay alive. Someone at school ratted on me, and the Martínez brothers, who were still little kids, swore they were going to kill me, but they couldn't do anything because I was older, and even if they weren't scared of me, all I had to say was: 'I'll get Víctor onto you. Whatcha gonna do about it, *motherfuckerth*?'

In any case, they'd got their own back and now we were even, but I couldn't let Mum find out, because she'd only see the old Melissa, and I didn't want to give her a reason to leave again. No, siree. That's why I hadn't asked her for the money for the printer. Like the Martínez brothers with their revenge, I had to play the long game. First, I needed Mum to realize I was a different person now.

I was nervous ringing Adela's doorbell, but when I went in nobody noticed the stain. Mum and Adela were busy having a good-natured argument they immediately drew me into.

'Ask her, ask your daughter,' said Adela, 'See what she says.'

'Ask me what?'

'Don't listen to her. Adela thinks I'm still fifteen years old, that's all.'

'Your mum thinks going out two nights in a row is too much. I never thought I'd see the day!' Adela looked at Mum again. 'You, Milena Flores, saying two nights in a row is too much. Come on, babe, don't think I've forgotten the time you had to be dragged out of Olivo at six in the morning!'

'Don't listen to her, Meli, your mother has always been a saint.'

'Oh, Milenita, not even you believe that,' Adela said, before turning to me. 'You'd go out tonight and tomorrow as well, right Melissa?'

'Course. Where are we going?'

'See, babe?' Adela cried. 'Like mother like daughter. It's decided, the three of us are going out tonight, then you guys can go to your party tomorrow.'

'What party?' I asked.

'A party at a friend's place. I wanted to take you both,' Mum replied, 'but because missy over here has to work tomorrow night, she's insisting we go out tonight as well.'

'So?' Adela asked.

Mum sighed.

'Fine,' she said. 'But not to Olivo.'

'Come on, babe, that place closed down years ago.'

'Really? Because of that disgusting drink?'

'Because it went bankrupt after you left town. But don't worry, I know somewhere even better. Right, then it's agreed, we'll start getting ready in an hour and then head out.'

As for me, I needed a shower. The warm water made my nose feel better, but when I got out I realized I didn't know what to wear. I sat on the sofa wrapped in a towel to go through everything I'd packed.

'When did you get that?'

I jumped at Mum's voice. I turned my head and saw her pointing at the silhouette of a deer tattooed on my shoulder.

'Three months ago, maybe,' I replied. 'You like it?'

'I love it! Where did you get it done?'

'This little place near Chapinero.'

'Do you still have their number?'

'You want another one?'

'Maybe, though Jorge doesn't like them much.'

'Jorge?' I asked, raising an eyebrow.

'A friend.'

'Is that what we're calling them now?'

'OK, OK,' she said, grabbing my hairbrush, which was on the coffee table. 'We're dating.'

'Dating?'

'Yeah...'

'Oh, come on, tell me! Is he from here or Bucaramanga?'

'From here, but I met him there,' she replied, brushing my hair.

'How long has it been? Is he hot? Do you have a photo?'

'God,' she let out a little laugh. 'It's been about eight months. And *hot* hot, I dunno, you can tell me what you think tomorrow.'

'Tomorrow? He's gonna be at the party?'

'It's at his house.'

That's how I knew I had to save my nicest outfit for tomorrow. Tonight, I'd wear the jeans I'd had on all day, with a furry waist-length jacket and a black choker I loved but which was a bit more nightclub than house party. You can be more creative in a club because it's darker and full of strangers.

I looked good that night – not amazing, but good. When I looked in the mirror, sometimes I thought I was pretty and sometimes that I was just good at faking it. I felt like, if someone stared too long or got too close, they'd figure out the ruse and start noticing all the crappy needlework, the patches, stains and rips, like an old shirt. Looking good is about covering up all the bad stuff, hiding it. Looking incredible is about making other people fall in love with those things.

Zapata always looked incredible at parties. She hardly ever wore make-up and barely brushed her hair, but she pulled it off. She wore weird clothes, old clothes, designer clothes, combinations that aren't supposed to work, which would make anyone else (me) look like a cross between a librarian and a street thief, but on her they were perfect. I don't know what her secret was. Maybe just that, no matter what she wore, she gave the impression she liked what she saw in the mirror. So others ended up liking it too.

Mum was wearing a black sequinned skirt and a loose, cream-coloured blouse with a slit on each shoulder. On one side, a bit of yellow ink from her Tweety tattoo peeped out. I realized that, without discussing it, we'd both ended up with tattoos in the same place. As well as that one, Mum had a tattoo of my name on her ankle in blue ink that used to be black. She liked that one, but she hated the Tweety. 'This year I'm finally getting rid of this disgusting thing, Meli,' she'd been saying since I was little. 'I really am, this year.' She never did, but instead found ways to cover it up, which was hard because Mum always used to dress like she was in Melgar, not Bogotá: tank tops, shorts, skirts, sometimes even sandals.

Whenever we walked round town we were dogged by whistles and shouts of 'sexy mama'. She never responded, just held my hand more tightly. It happened all the time, even to women like Karen's mum, who always dressed like she was going to mass, but with Mum the fuckers seemed bolder somehow. Sometimes they'd follow us for an entire block and once someone put his hand down her trousers on a bus. I don't remember how old I was when they started catcalling me too, I couldn't tell the difference.

The day of the hand down her trousers, Mum screamed. We were so squashed that there was nowhere to go, the guy was right there. I froze, no idea what to do. Mum went on yelling but nobody did anything. Finally, another man made his way through all the people and said something to the guy, who beat a path to the door. Mum went quiet after that, like nothing had happened, but as soon as we got home and shut the door she started crying. I wished I'd done something on the bus – I was so angry, I wanted to break the guy's face in. I wished I'd at least shouted at him. Dad would have done, I thought, but when Mum told him what happened he just went on watching TV. When she insisted, he just asked what she wanted, what she expected to happen when she went out of the house dressed like that.

She didn't reply, but she didn't start dressing differently either, not till now.

After that day, I decided I wasn't going to keep quiet anymore, no fucking way. I even practised answers in my head, like 'You're disgusting' or just 'Eat shit', but the next time we were catcalled I froze again. It was like a switch had been flicked: click, off. Only in the street, though. If anyone at school said anything to me, they got the shit beaten out of them for sure. What usually happened was I threw myself on them, then wham, right in the face, and if they tried to fight back, I'd yell, 'You can't hit a girl, you piece of shit!' That way it was clear no one was gonna take me for a ride, nope, not me.

I knew that when we went out people would catcall us no matter what, it didn't matter how much Mum changed what she wore. And that wasn't the only thing she'd changed – she'd also stopped smoking, barely swore anymore and was all round more chill. She used to give the impression she didn't want to stay anywhere, like she was always in a rush to meet someone who never showed up.

Mum really was pretty, she didn't have to fake it. Pretty in hot-weather clothes and pretty in ketchup-advert clothes. Pretty when her eyes were all swollen and pretty in long sleeves to hide her bruises, pretty dancing salsa round the kitchen. When she smiled, really smiled, it was impossible not to smile with her.

It was the first time we'd been out (or done anything) together in a long time, and I had to show her I'd changed too. That's why I didn't wait till the last minute to start getting ready. I wanted to be done on time – no, not just on time, I wanted to be ready first. While Adela was in the shower and Mum sat looking at her phone, still not dressed, I used the mirror in the living room to do my foundation and lipstick. I wanted to show Mum there'd be no problems today, at least not from me. Or rather, that I wasn't going to be a problem because I was no longer the kind of person who talked back or slammed doors or climbed out of the window or stole cigarettes or picked fights or broke into other people's houses. Though that was a one-time thing anyway.

I was with Dayana. I don't know how old we were, all I know is we still fit through Doña Nancy's windows. There were bars on them but there was loads of space between each one and Nancy left the window open during the day (for the plants, she said), and at night she forgot to shut it. We broke in just to see if we could and once we were in we decided we had to take something. On a little table in the living room, along with photo frames in various sizes, candles and flowerpots, there were these little silver trays. Well, not silver, silver-plated. At that age, everything silver was silver. The table was so crammed with stuff that I still think Doña Nancy wouldn't have even realized the trays were gone if I hadn't knocked over one of the flowerpots as I was climbing out of the window. Soil went everywhere, voices were heard. I bashed myself against the bars, but both Dayana and I managed to get out before anyone saw us. The whole neighbourhood found out about the burglary, but they never caught us. Though people suspected it had been me, Mum got furious whenever anyone suggested it. So furious that she really did seem convinced I'd had nothing to do with it. But she didn't look me in the eye for almost an entire month. She didn't punish me or say anything, but I'm sure she knew. The worst thing is, I'd have told her the truth if she'd asked. I'd have told her anything to get her to look at me again.

In front of the mirror, I realized my right eyebrow needed plucking. The swelling on my nose hadn't completely gone down, but you couldn't really tell under the make-up. I still had to do my eyes though. I'd brought (borrowed) one of Aunt Anahí's eyeliners. I wasn't used to using the liquid, but this one was so lovely I didn't care that I had to try several times before getting the line right. 'Rest your elbow on something, kid.' I tried to do it like Anahí had showed me. 'Put your little finger against your cheek. Slower,' she corrected me until she got bored and drew the line for me herself. She made it look so easy. Not just that, she also enjoyed doing it, even when she was making herself up in a rush before work. That's why she was so good at it. She'd probably spent years doing it in secret. Who knows, maybe she taught Mum how to do her make-up too, maybe she used to do her eyeliner the way she did mine.

It was Mum who told me about Aunt Anahí's change. Shame, because it would have been funnier if my aunt had told me. I know that when she told Aunt Magdalena she said: 'Your dream's come true, darling, I'm not going to be a gay boy anymore.' Maybe it would have been easier to understand if Mum had started with a joke. Probably not, it would probably have been more confusing, but funnier.

When Mum explained to me about Aunt Anahí, the first thing I thought was of Dad. I thought of his friends, the jokes they used to make about Uncle Roberto. I felt as bad as when I used to see them doing impressions of him and cracking up laughing. I hated that laughter because my own was mixed in with it. I laughed, of course I laughed, but my stomach would be in knots, because at that moment I was ashamed of Uncle Roberto, ashamed to have him as my uncle. I didn't want to feel that way because he didn't deserve it, and I was angry that I couldn't help it. I was angry with Uncle Roberto. Why couldn't he be easy to love, like other uncles? Easy to love openly. That was the first thing I felt when I heard what Mum had to say.

Please, please let no one round here find out, I begged quietly, over and over. Let nobody at school find out, let Karen and Dayana not find out, let no one in my year find out, not even Porky Pili, especially not her, because she'll throw it all back in my face. I panicked – but Mum was calm. What the fuck! I got angry. Sure, what did she have to lose? Nothing. Meanwhile, what about me? I'd started shouting, but then Mum held my hand like she did when Dad got difficult and told me that Uncle Roberto needed us. *Fuck me.* That threw me, because I could understand that part. 'He needs us and he's going to need us for a long time, Meli.' *Fuck me sideways.* Uncle Roberto had always been there for us, always waiting with open arms when we ran away in the middle of the night.

That feeling I had at the beginning slowly faded, especially because Mum was so calm. But then I started to get scared. Not scared that others in the neighbourhood would make fun of me, scared of losing my uncle. Scared he'd be gone forever. As he changed, I worried more and more that he'd fade until I only had memories of him left. That person I loved – because I did love him – would be gone forever. I thought it would be like seeing Uncle Roberto swimming out to sea until he was just a speck in the distance and then disappearing altogether.

Sometimes I thought Aunt Magdalena had the same fear. Maybe she was even more scared than me, that's why she didn't give herself the chance to see that distant speck reappear between the waves, swimming towards the shore as Aunt Anahí. The same person, but happy. Maybe it was harder for Aunt Magdalena because she felt like she'd lost her father twice. First her real father, then what was left of him in his only son. Maybe she thought one thing had caused the other. Maybe she was scared by the idea that a man, any man, but especially her brother, could stop being a man. Who knows, maybe not. Maybe none of that was the problem, maybe even she didn't know what the problem was. I probably spent longer than her wondering what her problem was, so if I didn't know, she definitely didn't.

It scared me a bit, too – the idea that a man could stop being a man. It meant the same could happen to women, which meant me. And I was scared that it might happen to me without me realizing, that one day someone would look at me and point and say, 'Look, a girl who punches people!' or, 'Look, a girl who doesn't cry!' and someone would reply, 'Don't worry, that's not a girl,' and then I'd stop being one. I didn't want to stop punching people or start crying, but I didn't want to be a boy either. The boys in my class were gross. I thought that maybe, if I dressed like a woman, like the women in the magazines, with my hair all nicely done, make-up and heels, I could get away with not behaving like one. I realized the men in our neighbourhood shouted at women regardless, the women who dressed like in the magazines and the women who didn't, all women. In the end, make-up and clothes didn't matter at all. Being a woman means not being able to go out into the street without being catcalled.

I waited for Mum and Adela, dressed and made-up half an hour early. My fingers had seized up and my left eye was a bit red, but no one could deny that the eyeliner looked fucking great. A perfect line. I wished Anahí was there so I could show off. Even though we were in a fight, she'd have to admit I'd done a spectacular job. And I'd smile and say, 'I'll teach you, if you like, any time.'

'Woweee, don't you look gorgeous,' Mum said on our way out the door, as I did a little twirl to show off my look.

It was cold outside, but as soon as we went into La Pinta I regretted bringing a jacket. I thought I was going to have to carry it round all night, but there was a cloakroom where Adela also left her coat. They put them in a black bin bag marked with a number written in masking tape and gave us a ticket that Adela tucked into her bra. The club was narrow and you had to swim through crowds of people to get anywhere, but at least there was a free bar. Mum ordered Bacardi.

'Your mum used to drink that with condensed milk,' Adela said, leaning on the bar.

'Ew, condensed milk?' I asked, looking at Mum. From the way she started laughing it was clear she really had.

We were passed three disposable cups. Not the ones you buy in the supermarket, these were sturdier and somewhere between indigo and navy blue, or at least in the nightclub lighting they were, a colour that reminded me of the sea in Pilar Villareal's school project.

We were in Year Three or Four and had to make a model, using recycled materials, of a scene from *Treasure Island*. The best model would win a prize – a lollypop or a chocolate bar or something. At that age any piece of crap can be a prize. The important thing, the thing that really mattered, was going home and telling Mum that I'd been awarded something (besides a telling-off).

Pilar arrived that day with a beautiful model, so big she could barely carry it. It had sand and real shells and a sea made of layers of paint, glitter and cellophane to look like waves. In the middle, under palm trees like the ones in nativity scenes, were a bunch of little figures. One even had a parrot on its shoulder, printed onto a piece of paper. It was obvious she hadn't used anything recycled and that her parents had done it for her, but it was without a doubt the best model in the class. I had nothing. I'd forgotten to make one.

That's what I told everyone, that I'd forgotten. The truth was I'd actually started working on one days earlier. I used cereal boxes and rolls of toilet paper painted this old green colour that was closer to brown. I spent two whole afternoons trying to finish it but everything I did only made it worse. I destroyed it the same way I destroyed Pilar's: by kicking it.

I kicked one because it was pretty and the other because it was ugly. Both were a kind of punishment. Yes, I punished

Pilar, because despite her not making it herself, and using new materials that cost God knows how much (much more than what the prize was worth), the teachers were going to let her win. And I punished her for shaming my own attempt at building a model. I hated her project because I hated mine and I hated mine so much that I had to destroy it twice, would have destroyed it three times, four, if I'd had the opportunity. None of the teachers realized it was me who broke Pilar's and when they asked if anyone knew anything – Pilar was crying at the front of the classroom – I raised my hand and said that Porky Pili had probably sat on it.

'Ew, that was gross,' I said, wrinkling my nose.

As the Bacardi went down I felt the urge to throw up.

The second one was better, but not much. I hardly ever drank rum, especially not white rum, but – according to Adela – it was Mum's favourite drink. Aunt Anahí sometimes drank wine, and some evenings she liked to open the living room window and smoke a cigarette. Katya would curl up next to her on the sofa and sometimes I'd do the same. She almost always ended up watching some black-and-white film, which I probably would have liked too, but mainly liked falling asleep to. I was used to drinking whatever I could get, which meant guaro. I wouldn't say it was my favourite thing in the world, but it was cheap and achieved the desired effect. Beer was good, but I was scared of ending up with a huge belly like the men who drank outside Señor Héctor's.

The first time I got drunk it was on whisky. Dayana's parents were going away for the weekend and we'd been plotting since Monday. It was about two months before I left Corpus Cristi, because I remember us laughing about it afterwards, at my leaving party. Dayana said her cousin Manuel could get a bottle of guaro for us. It wasn't going to be a party exactly, something smaller, more chill.

'Great, so it'll be Víctor, you, me, Karen and Junior,' said Dayana, as we made the list in Spanish class.

'Ooh!' I cried, I guess too loudly, because the teacher looked up. I ducked, before whispering: 'I know, I know, let's invite Dylan.'

'You think he'll come?'

'Let me do it, I'll convince him, but we can't tell Karen or she'll be a nervous wreck all week. How many is that?'

'Six. Who else? Mariana?'

'Umaña or Torres?'

'Umaña.'

'No, Torres, Umaña's insufferable now that she's got big tits. And we'll have to invite a friend of Dylan's. What's that pale kid called?'

'Lucho?'

'Him.'

The idea was to invite enough people so that when we were back at school on Monday people would be talking about it, but not so many that everyone would know what had really gone on. Dylan was in the year above, so if he came it meant he was into Karen. I bit my lip so I wouldn't scream when he said yes, but I didn't tell Karen until Friday when we were getting ready. Actually, we didn't even tell her, she figured out by herself that something was going on because Dayana and I kept redoing her make-up and hair. She went bright red.

'No no no,' she said, shaking her head.

'Yes, and it's obvious he has a crush on you,' Dayana told her.

'What should I say to him?'

'Nothing,' I said. 'Just be chill. Don't go and find him, let him come to you.'

'Let him come…' she repeated.

'But you have to keep giving him the look.'

'Look… what kind of look?'

'She's going to pass out on us,' Dayana laughed. 'Time for a shot.'

But that fucker Manuel hadn't come through with the booze. 'He's not picking up,' Dayana said, her phone clamped to her ear.

'Oh God, what if Dylan arrives and there's nothing to drink? No, no, let's cancel and do it another time.'

'No way, keep calling,' I told Dayana. 'It's still early.'

But by about half past eight Manuel was still nowhere to be seen. I asked Dayana if her parents had anything. We had a look and of course found a big half-empty bottle of whisky. Dayana took a bit of convincing, but not much, because I was still saying we wouldn't even drink half of what was left in the bottle when she'd already got the glasses out. We turned on the radio. It was Friday so there were long chunks of good music with hardly any ads. The three of us sat in the living room.

'Don't you like it?' Dayana asked Karen.

Karen was wrinkling her nose, curling her lip like when

Katya gets a whiff of nail varnish. It made me laugh so much I almost spat my drink out.

'No... yeah, it's... good...'

'Do us a favour, get her a chaser,' I said to Dayana, slapping her on the shoulder until she got up.

'It's good,' I said, as if I knew anything at all about whisky, before taking another sip.

'Sprite or Colombiana?' Dayana shouted from the kitchen, 'Or Pepsi?'

'Whatever!' I replied, 'But not Quatro! Anything but fucking Quatro.'

Karen laughed because about a month ago Dayana had got the idea to mix the guaro and beer she'd mineswept after one of her parent's parties in Quatro bottles and sneak it into the cinema. The concoction was so disgusting I hadn't been able to drink Quatro since.

'You're both such drama queens,' Dayana said, returning with a two-litre bottle of Colombiana. 'It was pretty good, I thought.'

'Even you didn't finish it!'

'All right, all right! No more complaining or I'm not giving you anything. *Nena, nena, tranquilícese*,' she sang along to the radio as she poured out more whisky, '*que en la calle a nadie besé*. Pass your glass, Noriega, don't just sit there. *Que pena me daría no tenerte en mi vida, vida mía*.'

'After tonight, this will be your and Dylan's song, Karencita. Fill me up, come on, you call that a drink?'

'Can't our song be something that's not reggaeton?'

'What's wrong with reggaeton? That's how Víctor asked me out.'

'I would have said no just because of that,' said Dayana, and I whacked her playfully round the head.

'Don't overthink it, Karencita,' I said. 'Ask him out tonight when this song's playing.'

'What, you're crazy,' replied Karen. 'It's got to be to "Mayor que yo."'

The three of us laughed. By the time Manuel arrived with two boxes of guaro, the bottle of whisky was almost gone and we had to fill it up with water from the shower because it wouldn't fit in any of the sinks.

By the fourth Bacardi, I started to feel that drunken heat. Like I was dipping my brain in a bucket of warm water. I knew it was taking effect because I was singing along to songs I didn't know, but it didn't matter, the music was good. I'd been wanting them to put salsa on for ages, not to dance so much as to watch Mum dance. We'd got ourselves into a group of strangers and everyone clapped when Adela went into the middle and got down so low she practically grazed the floor before coming up again. After someone took her off for a dance, Mum and I went to the bar for more cocktails. The lights were painting her face different colours.

Green.

'How you doing? You good, Meli?'

Red.

'Yeah, yeah, all good.'

'Passionfruit or strawberry?'

Purple.

'What?'

'Passionfruit or strawberry cocktail?'

Blue.

'Passionfruit.'

After ordering she looked at me again. I looked back at her. I'd forgotten she had a mole above her lip, or maybe it was new. She passed me the cup.

'Here you go, love.'

Why did you leave, Mum?

Green.

I took a long swig, to see if it would make the urge to ask questions fade away. Passionfruit and rum. I didn't like it, the strawberry one was better. I finished it anyway. I told Mum I needed the toilet and she said she'd come with me.

As we pushed our way through people, a guy grabbed me for a dance. He appeared out of nowhere and was spinning me round before I'd even got a look at his face. I tried to move away, but he grabbed my hand and pulled me in again. I hadn't quite fully understood why I was suddenly dancing, so I just said 'toilet', and tried to get away again. 'Eh?' he said, coming closer to hear better. Then Mum got involved, putting an arm round my shoulders without a word, and the guy finally let me go. I remembered how nice it felt to have Mum looking after me.

In the bathroom there were four women queuing in front of the sinks. People were only going into one cubicle, the other door was shut and there were no signs of life from in there. I was tempted to push it open, but thought better of it, because someone might have vomited in there. While we were in the queue, Mum stared at me. I wondered if she was figuring out that the drink had started to hit me, and whether she'd be annoyed, but she smiled.

'You're so tall,' she said.

'It's the heels.'

She laughed.

'You look like...'

Like you?

'Like who?'

'No, nothing. You won't like it.'

'Now you have to tell me!' I insisted. 'You can't stop now.'

'Like your Aunt Magdalena, when she was your age.'

'Noooo!' The word slipped out before I could stop myself.

'She's pretty.'

'Only on the outside.'

That also slipped out, and I looked worriedly at Mum, because I didn't know if I'd said something bad. I mean, I was pretty sure she agreed with me, but Magda was her sister and maybe that wasn't the kind of thing you wanted to hear about your sister (I wouldn't know, I didn't have one), and besides, I was tipsy, and I tended to say stupid things when I was tipsy. I was about to backtrack when Mum spoke.

'Don't say anything to her,' she whispered, 'but she changed so much after she married Alfredo.'

That 'don't say anything to her' echoed round my head. She didn't need to ask, I never talked to Aunt Magda, and even if I did, I obviously wouldn't say anything, but I liked the air of secrecy, of confidence. I liked it a lot. It was a novelty. Now that I wasn't a kid anymore, she could tell me that kind of thing, maybe start filling in the gaps in the stories I knew, talking about what happened between them, maybe even talking about Dad.

'I think Aunt Magda is too old.'

Mum looked confused by this, and I realized half the idea had got stuck in my head.

'Too old to be scared, I mean.'

'Scared?' Mum asked.

'Of Aunt Anahí. No, not of her. Of… of a man no longer being a man, you know what I mean?'

She was thoughtful for a moment, then asked: 'What about you?'

'I'm scared of Aunt Magda. That woman's genuinely scary. Someone should warn her.'

'She'll figure it out herself, sooner or later.'

She didn't sound very convinced. Sad, rather, a bit hopeless.

'Sometimes people change,' I said, wanting her to understand we were actually talking about me now.

She smiled, but was still thoughtful. When it was finally my turn to go into the cubicle, I wished I hadn't. It was completely filthy, the bin overflowing and the floor covered in balls of used paper. The toilet doesn't even bear mentioning. When I came out, I looked at myself in the mirror. *Yeesh, that eyeliner's got away from you, princess*. A few people in the queue laughed and that's how I realized I'd said it out loud. That was the end of my perfect line.

I decided to wait for Mum outside the bathroom, so as not to be in the way. Just then, a woman came past handing out guaro. She passed me a brimming shot glass. I downed it and everyone nearby cheered. *Never accept drinks from strange men, Melissa*, I scolded myself. *Strange women, though, that's all right.* Bad joke, but I made myself laugh before handing back the little empty glass. A guy took me off for a dance. He had a pretty face and looked about twenty, though in that light it was hard to tell. Venezuelan. I don't know which city. His hands moved further and further down my back.

Fucking Dylan turned up at one in the morning with his arm round another girl's shoulders. I couldn't believe my eyes. I was going to give him a piece of my mind, I wouldn't let him treat Karen like that. But then the idiot disappeared. Someone told me he'd locked himself in the room upstairs with the new girl. I ran up as fast as I could. The bedroom door was locked. I knocked. No answer, but they were clearly in there. I kicked the door. 'Open up! Open the cocksucking motherfucking door!' I said. Where was Karen? Crying in a corner. Víctor? Outside smoking. Dayana? Who knows. 'If I have to knock the door down, I will, I'll knock this fucking door down.' And I kicked even harder, and punched, punched, punched, harder, punch, then I heard it. I swear I heard it. Like stepping on a branch. I didn't scream yet, not till I saw my right thumb. The door was intact, but my thumb had swollen up like a potato, purple and black.

Next thing I knew I was kneeling next to the toilet bowl. For a second, I thought nothing had happened, that I'd imagined it all, but my throat hurt and I felt like my thumb was sitting on a stovetop. It was boiling hot and heavy. 'She's broken it, it looks broken—' 'No, it's not broken, it's sprained—' 'We should call... we should go to the hospital' 'She's drunk' 'We should— not the hospital...' 'Fuckssake, Noriega, all that fighting and you don't even know how to throw a punch...' I didn't want anyone near me because I was scared they'd touch my thumb. Later, we were in a car. I didn't realize it was a taxi until Víctor paid. 'How are you feeling?' asked Karen, sitting next to me. 'Can you walk?' Inside, the white light made me feel sick. The waiting room was full, Víctor and Karen were standing, pacing up and down, and I was sitting. *What if they cut it off? What if they cut it off?*

We started dancing closer. He worked at Plaza Paloquemao, in a shop belonging to his uncle, who'd come to Colombia two years before. Over the noise of the music, he thought I said I was at university and instead of correcting him I said, yeah, I was doing business admin.

The bad news: it was broken. The good news: it didn't need surgery. They put a cast on quickly, and the doctor was finishing up when the nurse came back. She shook her head.

'The line's dead.' She said. 'Is there another number I can call?'

Another number? She wants another fucking number? I didn't even know if my Dad was in the country and she wanted another number. I felt like screaming, screaming at her, but by this time I'd figured out I needed to get her on side if I was going to get out of there. So I shook my head and asked her to try my mum again. They weren't going to let me out unless someone came to pick me up.

'I can call my aunts.'

'It has to be your parents,' the doctor informed me.

I looked at the nurse. She dialled the landline while I dialled Mum's mobile from my own phone. *Pick up, pick up*, I begged as it was ringing.

'If not,' the nurse murmured to the doctor, 'we'll have to call Social Services.'

Please pick up.

I kissed him first. They started playing merengue. I asked him if people danced merengue in Venezuela too. He said of course, and picked up the pace as though to prove it. There were a couple of drops of sweat on his forehead, but I didn't care. I was sweating, too.

Karen and Víctor were still in the waiting room. I showed them the cast on my thumb and they were the first to sign it for me. I told them I had to stay until my mum arrived and Víctor tried to convince the nurse to let me leave with him. 'I can call my mum,' he said, 'she can sign or… do whatever needs doing.' He was so lovely, Víctor, he knew his mum would kill him if he called her in the middle of the night to come and get him from hospital, but he'd have taken the hit for me. The nurse said it wasn't possible. I told them not to worry, Mum was on her way. I kept insisting until they left. The next day, I told them that Mum had turned up and we'd gone to the nearest Lindi's for chips and that I'd told her everything.

*

'I like this song,' I shouted, though we were so close it wasn't necessary. 'They played it at my graduation, at the party.'

'Cool,' he replied, and we kissed again. 'I was top of my class.' He congratulated me. 'Beauty and brains,' he said, and I just laughed. Dancing with strangers has its charms.

Only half of what I told them was a lie. Mum and I did go to Lindi's but I didn't tell her anything, I refused to speak to her, and it wasn't the middle of the night but rather the next day that she picked me up from Social Services.

I'd have danced with him a while longer, but they marked the end of the merengue cycle with a Joe Arroyo salsa and I ran off to find Mum. I wanted to see her dance. I searched the crowds, shouting 'Milena! Milena!' It felt weird using her name, but I didn't want to shout 'Mum!' in the club. I might be drunk, but I still had my dignity. I saw her raise an arm to wave me over.

I made my way towards her and she took my hand to dance. And suddenly she was in her element, as though her arms and legs and hands were dictating the notes of the song, as though they were writing it. And I was four years old again in our kitchen, waiting for the cake to come out of the oven. She spun me round once, twice, little step to the side, another to the back, we linked arms then unlinked them as though it was the simplest thing, movements I'd never made before but that felt natural with her leading me.

'I didn't know I could dance like this,' I said, and had to repeat it a couple of times for her to hear me.

'The apple doesn't fall far from the tree,' slurred Adela, who'd come back from God only knows where.

'Not far at all,' Mum said, and twirled me round, making the whole club spin.

I didn't care about feeling dizzy, the only thing that mattered was the way Mum had said *Not far at all.*

Around three in the morning they played Juan Gabriel to try and start getting rid of us. I sang along to the whole thing, even the bits I didn't know. We ended up hugging strangers, holding our drinks in the air as though toasting all our awful exes. Mum put an arm round my shoulders and pulled me into her chest for a hug. She said something, I couldn't hear what, and when I asked her to say it again she couldn't hear me. A stranger tried to kiss me, but I pushed him away, *No, dickhead, not in front of Mum.* The guy invited me to his flat, supposedly for an afterparty, but I didn't even respond, heading instead for the exit with Mum and Adela. It was all right to be drunk, but not stupid. It had been raining outside, who knows for how long, and while we waited for the bus it started coming down more heavily. I was so sweaty that the water running down my forehead and cheeks actually felt nice.

We were soaked through by the time we got back to Adela's. My hair was dripping, my top clung to my ribs, my jacket weighed triple what it was supposed to, my trousers were chafing and I was shaking with cold. Adela fell into bed at once, so Mum took charge of getting towels out and making hot chocolate. I could barely walk straight, so I sat down on the sofa bed and started taking my wet clothes off. Mum dried my hair with a towel, carefully squeezing out the water. She wrapped me in another towel and asked where my pyjamas were.

'Grey T-shirt,' I replied, my eyelids heavy, 'the one with the kangaroo.'

'This?'

I nodded.

'Get yourself properly dry and put it on.'

She came back with hot chocolate. My hair was still dripping but I was starting to warm up now I had dry pyjamas on. We sat down to drink the hot chocolate, while outside the birds were starting to sing. It was still dark and rain was beating on the ledge outside. Mum put a hand on my forehead. It was cold. I was drunk.

'God, I hope you don't end up with a temperature.'

'I like, I like having a temperature…'

'What?'

'At school, a temperature meant I could go home… and we'd spend the whole day together… Remember? I didn't have to go to school.'

'Course I remember.'

'It's been ages since…'

'Since what?'

'Ages since we… ages since we saw each other.' I knew, knew I was on the verge of asking, that I really was going to do it this time, because all the reasons I hadn't done it earlier had dissolved with the last of the cocktails. 'Why?'

She sighed slowly and deeply. I looked at the hot chocolate, swirled the mug slowly to cool it down a bit, and as I watched the bubbles on top disappear, I remembered that the real reason I hadn't asked earlier was that I didn't want to hear the reply.

'Meli,' she sighed again, and I went on staring at my hot chocolate. 'I… I'm so sorry I didn't come for such a long time. I know I haven't… that there are a lot of things I could have done better.'

She reached out her hand and tucked a lock of hair behind my ear. It had fallen over my eyes but I'd left it there because my hands were busy with the mug.

'But now everything's going to be different, better. I mean it, I'm sorting everything out so I can come back to Bogotá.'

I looked up to see if she was serious.

'And when I'm back,' she finished, 'I'd like for you to come and live with me.'

SUNDAY

Everything comes to an end, apparently – *Todo tiene su final*, as the Héctor Lavoe song goes. But Don Héctor obviously never had to go to 8 a.m. mass on a hangover. The priest's voice tuned in and out, like a kind of buzzing, giving me the heebie-jeebies every time his lips came too close to the microphone so you could hear his tongue, like a dog lapping up water. Eurgh. To top it all off, I was standing, because I'd been all polite, all, No no no, don't worry at all, señora, take my seat, please. *Well done, Melissa, very nice and considerate and all, but now you're fucked for the next hour.* Mum and Adela were sitting in the last row of benches and I was standing behind them. Mum had her eyes shut and her head forwards, still as a little shepherd in a nativity scene. She didn't even look like she was breathing. I was surprised by her concentration.

'Don't look at me,' Adela said that morning when they woke me up to invite me to mass. 'It was her idea.'

Since when does she go to church? I don't remember her taking me even once. Mum couldn't even sit through Holy Week films. I remember she made me change the channel during one once – there was a wife telling her husband to lie with the slave woman because she couldn't give him a son herself, and the husband says all right, if that is God's wish (only if God wishes it, though, right matey?) and, well, no prizes for guessing whether he does or not. It was odd, Mum changing the channel, because worse things happened in telenovelas shown in the middle of the day, but she liked those, loved them. Maybe Grandma and Grandad had forced her to watch those films when she was little, or maybe something about the way they talked about the slave woman was too close to the way the neighbourhood men shouted at her, too much like Dad.

I didn't mind the Holy Week films: they had their charm. Jesus turning water into wine, a classic moment, and the Last Supper, that was always the best part. Maybe I liked it because it was just a group of friends, together for the last time. Jesus knew what was going to happen, Judas knew what was going to happen, we all knew what was going to happen and still, I guess it was kind of nice watching them break bread and all that for the last time. Yeah, I liked that even though they all knew things were about to go to shit, they were able to have a moment of happiness.

'Why betrayal?' asked Zapata once, in catechism class.

'Sorry?' asked the teacher, Olguita, surprised. Nobody ever participated in her class (nobody paid enough attention).

'Judas is the worst, right?' said Zapata. 'The worst of the worst, pure evil. And that was his worst sin, wasn't it? Betrayal. But why is it the worst sin?'

'Well, betrayal is… not good.'

'But sometimes it is, right? Like converted saints. They betrayed their previous religion.'

I looked at Zapata to see if she was being serious or just wanted to fuck with Olguita. I wasn't sure, but now everyone was paying attention. Zapata had managed to wipe the smile off the teacher's face. The poor woman was looking worried, furrowing her brow, pursing her lips.

'Conversion is not a betrayal,' Olguita responded drily.

'What about Peter, then.'

'What?'

'Peter also betrayed Jesus, right?'

'Peter denied Jesus, he didn't betray him.'

'No?'

'No.'

'So who decides what's betrayal and what isn't?'

'Well, the Bible.'

Olguita got redder and redder and what was left of the class slipped out of her control as she tried to insist that Judas really was a sinner and that betrayal really was bad, going all the way back to Cain and Abel and the serpent and the apple. She trembled with rage, biting her lip so as not to let out a 'stupid child', while Zapata just would not give up. I thought it was a dare, that she'd said it all to wind Olguita up, but a couple of days later, out of nowhere, she brought up the topic again, when it was just the two of us.

'Olguita doesn't know.'

'What?'

'It isn't the betrayal, it's the thirty pieces of silver.'

'You still on about that, Zapatico?'

'Look, if Jesus's whole thing is love thy neighbour and all that, and Judas is, like, his opposite, why would the opposite of love be betrayal? The opposite of betrayal is loyalty, right, Norieguis? I think they're different, loyalty and love, but selling your neighbour out, that really is the opposite of love, don't you think? It's the thirty pieces of silver.'

'I dunno, Zapata, I don't really care about all that stuff… but anyway, isn't hate the opposite of love?'

'Yeah but there's no hate in the betrayal, the hate's in the silver. Otherwise, why would they give the keys to Peter? Because that really was a betrayal… Denying someone like that is betrayal, how could it not be? Peter was even worse than Judas because he was Jesus's best mate and he didn't deny him just once or twice, he denied him three times.'

'Where's all this coming from, Zapata?'

'I think I cheated on Cami… but I can't remember.'

'At Lu Gutiérrez's party?'

'Yeah, when I was dancing…'

'No, you didn't do anything.'

'No?'

'I was dancing right there too. Nothing happened.'

'Really?'

I nodded. Zapata sighed in relief. The truth was, I hadn't seen her and didn't know if she'd cheated or not, but if nobody remembered, what did it matter? What was the point of blaming yourself for something when, at the end of the day, it made no difference if it had happened or not? Zapata liked Cami, Cami liked Zapata, and I didn't want them to fight over something stupid. Zapata gave me a smile.

'I still think I'm right about Judas.'

*

And since when the fuck do I go to church? I thought, looking at the black-and-white chequered tiles, before the priest said we could sit down. Since today, I guess. But I couldn't have chosen a worse day to start. Not only did I have a headache and a dry throat, it was also one of those mornings when I'd woken up feeling like crying for no reason.

It happened every now and then, ever since I was little in Corpus Cristi, but also at Aunt Anahí's. I'd wake up with this kind of mewling trapped in my chest. Sometimes it was so powerful that the only way I could get out of bed was to repeat, over and over, that for the whole rest of the day I wasn't going to feel any worse than this (which was almost always true). And bit by bit, as I had a shower, breakfast, the whole routine, the need to cry would slowly disappear.

In the church I thought I saw a couple of familiar faces, but there were others I didn't recognize who stared at me. What were they saying? Were they leaning over to their husbands and whispering, 'Is that Milena's girl?' Did the men pretend to look before giving a shrug, then at the end of mass the women would say, Yes, yes, it was her, she looks so different, do you remember how awful she was, apparently they had her sent to juvenile detention.

That thing I used to get in the mornings, the thing that made me feel like crying, it wasn't sadness. Sadness is that film about the dog who goes every day to the train station to wait for his dead owner. Sadness is a night alone in Social Services. Sadness is understandable. This was… nothingness, a vacuum. I know what sadness is, what causes it, but this? The vacuum feeling would arrive even when nothing bad had happened, even when nothing hurt, nothing. Sometimes I thought maybe it was like the leak in Aunt Anahí's dining room. The pain was somewhere else, or hadn't happened yet – something had gone wrong in the flat upstairs and little bits of sadness were dripping down onto me in the present.

I looked around, searching for the faces of Pilar Villareal's parents. I sort of remembered her dad, a bald, brown-skinned guy with big lips. I don't remember her mum though. Maybe they didn't go to mass. I don't know why I wanted to see them, maybe to tell them I'd dreamed about their daughter. It hadn't been a bad dream: we were in school, Corpus Cristi District School, except the buildings were Ofelia's. We had to do a presentation together, a poster. That was all, but I woke up with that vacuum. Fuckssake. *Why'd I have to wake up wanting to cry in someone else's fucking house.* I didn't often remember my dreams before I woke up with that feeling, which is why it wasn't until that morning, at Adela's, that it occurred to me maybe the feeling didn't come from something that hadn't happened yet but rather from something that had already happened. Maybe that's why I was looking for them at mass.

When the smell of incense collided with my hangover I worried I might throw up, so had to leave the church. I whispered to Mum that I needed some fresh air and left. When I stepped out into the street, I still intended to go back, but then I started walking and by the time I got to the end of the block I realized I was on my way to Pilar Villareal's house. I had to find her. I had to see her, to know if she was real, that it had all been real.

I knew the way.

I don't think Karen was there that time, because that sort of thing was more mine and Dayana's territory. We knew Karen would say something or at least have that look about her, like a lamb before the slaughter. Better to leave her out of it.

Pilar never did anything to me. I said she stole my lunch box once, which was true for the ten minutes it took her to realize she'd confused it with her own. She never did anything to me, she didn't even defend herself, and that only made me angrier. I wanted to be provoked, to be given a reason.

Dayana would follow my lead, but these things were never her idea. We'd already thrown eggs at her house once, but this time we went armed with blue spray paint, like Millonarios fans. The thing is, it was so easy – you could yell anything at Pilar. Who was going to say anything? I could shout at her to shut up in the middle of class and no one would do anything, not even the teachers… the fucking teachers. What was their deal? Were they scared of me too? It was like it wasn't their problem, like they thought there was nothing they could do. We graffitied the whole front of the building, the windows, the door. Even if she didn't live on the ground floor, she still had to go in, there was no way she wouldn't see it. Over and over, in big wonky letters, in blue paint that dripped slowly and clumsily down the wall, we wrote 'PORKY PILI' 'FAT BITCH' 'KILL YOURSELF'.

I stopped when I saw the front of the building. It had been painted over, of course, but I thought you could still see a bit of blue, like when your pen goes through to the next page in a notebook. Karen had said they still lived there.

Why haven't they moved?

My hands were sweating. I started to feel like the whole street was spinning, like someone had put me in a blender. I felt an urge to run. Nobody had to know I'd bottled it. That I hadn't been able to look Pilar Villareal in the eye and say – say what?

I'm sorry.

It was the only thing there was to say. What else? There was nothing else, there was nothing else at all.

I felt sick, hungover. *I'd know, though.* I'd know I'd run away, that I'd bottled it. I didn't want to ring that bell. What if only her parents were in. I nibbled the cuticle on my thumb. *I should apologize to them too.* I had to leave. Quickly. This felt worse than going into a Social Science final. I could feel the teacher's marker pen tapping a thousand miles an hour, like a beating heart. 'It's not that fucking hard, Noriega.' My feet didn't move. I rang the doorbell. I was sweating. Had it rung? I could still run away.

'Hello?'

'Is Pilar Villareal there?'

She didn't recognize my voice.

'That's me.'

Nor I hers.

One time, Mum and I went to the beach with Aunt Magdalena, Alfredo and my cousins. It was a disaster. Obviously, we were supposed to be grateful to my aunt, who paid for pretty much the whole thing, but their banged-up old car conked out every time it tried to go uphill. Alfredo said it had air conditioning but when he turned it on the car gained a wet-dog smell, which lingered even after he turned it off. Juanchi and I argued about the music. Well, it started with the music, but then it got ugly. Juanchi insisted on playing a Santiago Cruz album, as if all his songs weren't just the same thing over and over, sung by someone with a blocked nose. It was doctor's waiting room music, not holiday music, but Juanchi went on and on about it because he'd learned the songs on his guitar. That's how it started. It ended with me giving him a Chinese burn on his arm. He cried (of course) and that only made me angrier. Then Aunt Magdalena got involved and started telling me off, which meant Mum got involved to defend me, and they ended up yelling at each other. Things had been getting worse and worse between them for a while.

I didn't even know half of what had happened, all I knew was it had something to do with money, with Grandad's flat, and that in the end the thing that properly pushed them apart was Aunt Anahí. At first, Mum would make excuses for Magdalena, in the same voice she made excuses for me. She told Anahí: 'You just have to be patient with her', 'It's a big change, she's getting used to it', 'She didn't mean it like that', 'She didn't mean to, not really.' Very patient, my mum, but Aunt Magda ended up scaring her, too.

The three of them went round and round in circles over Grandad's will. Aunt Anahí said something about Juanchi's birthday and Aunt Magdalena exploded. She said Anahí was sick and perverted, and not to even dream of going near her children because she'd call the police on her, that if she really cared about family she'd check herself into a clinic. Who knows what else she said, I'm sure Mum didn't tell me the worst of it. I said thank God I wasn't there because I'd have given Aunt Magda 'a good smack in the face'. Mum told me off but she didn't talk to Magdalena again for about two years. Anahí swore not to speak to her ever again.

So I don't know how we ended up trapped, Mum and I, on the way to the beach in that car that stank of dog with Aunt Magdalena, Alfredo and my cousins. Rosita vomited all over herself about an hour after I hurt Juanchi, as a form of revenge. 'She returned the favour,' Aunt Anahí would have said, if she'd been invited. At least she didn't return it on me, because then I would have been furious, properly furious, and would have returned *that* favour with my fists. And if I had, Mum and Aunt Magda would have had a proper catfight. We arrived and no one said anything. The hotel was ugly as hell, with no pool. I calculated how many hours were left before we could go home to Bogotá. I was desperate to get out of there – that is, until I saw the beach.

What a thing. The vast sea stretching out, the seagulls, the sound of the palm trees, the warm sand. Since we hadn't unpacked, we didn't have our swimsuits on, but my cousins and I ran to dip our feet in. Before long we were in up to our waists, laughing as the waves pushed us around. I thought Aunt Magdalena was going to tell us off for getting our clothes wet but when I looked for her on the beach I saw her in the distance, walking with Mum. The two of them were walking together, their shoes in their hands, bare feet leaving prints on the damp sand. They were talking. I didn't know what about, but right then everything else had disappeared, the dodgy car, the money trouble, the arguments, it was all gone, they were just two sisters by the sea. That's all. It might not seem like it often anymore, but there, in that moment, that's what they were. And I thought, maybe one day Aunt Anahí could talk to the two of them like that, to Aunt Magda. And maybe that day, Aunt Magda might say she was sorry.

Because there are conversations that are meant to be had that way. That are meant to be started when the sun is bouncing off the water and the beach vendors are doing the rounds, yelling about how tasty their cocadas are. Conversations that blot out the sunbathers and the children playing volleyball and end when the sky is purple and all you can hear is the sea and the sun has sunk into the water without you even realizing. The conversation I needed to have with Pilar was one of those.

So how was I supposed to talk to her there, on the side of the dirty street, on the steps stained black where the rainwater had run down towards the drain? How could I talk to her in Corpus Cristi, outside the same building where I'd written that she should die? No, not that she should die, that she should kill herself. I should at least have brought her something… Like what? Something, anything. I can't, I can't do it. I managed to take one step down. I almost slipped. I breathed. I stretched out my fingers like I'd just had my nails done and saw that I was shaking. I can't, not like this. Better do it another day. I looked at the door. It's now or never. I heard footsteps. Better never. She opened the door.

I didn't recognize her at first.

She stopped. She did recognize me, and took one step back.

I kept my eyes on her, but I started picking at the cuticle on my index finger with my thumb.

She'd dyed her hair blonde, almost silvery, with light-blue tips. It was lovely. Her hair was tangled and loose on the shoulders of her grey jacket. She was thin, very thin. Thin because of me? So that nobody could ever again compare her to a pig? She looked like she'd just got up. What time was it? I thought that, on seeing me, she'd turn around, go back inside and slam the door. Maybe I wanted her to. Instead, she looked me up and down and was the first to speak.

'What are you doing here?'

'I was in town...'

'What do you want?'

'I... well... I...'

She looked at me in silence. Impatiently.

'I... I thought that... well, that I'd come and...'

I had to stop beating around the bush. I took the plunge.

'To say sorry.'

'Sorry?'

'Yes.'

'No,' she said, shaking her head. 'No.'

'No?'

'I don't accept your apology.'

I stood motionless, silent. I'd thought the hardest part was over. I'd said it. I, who had never said it to anybody, who would never have said it when we were at school, had gone to her house specifically to say it. Instead of running, instead of turning round, I'd made a huge effort to say it, and I'd been so bent on saying it that it hadn't even occurred to me she might simply reject it.

'What did you expect?' she asked. 'A kiss on the forehead and to be invited in for breakfast?'

I was sweating. It was so hot. I looked at my hand. My skin was throbbing and there were little smears of blood where I'd ripped off my cuticle. It was time to leave, but before I could move, she spoke.

'I do want you to tell me why, though.'

'Why?' I repeated.

'Why did you ruin my life?'

She came down a step – just one, so I'd still have to look up to meet her eyes, to look at her at all, though at that precise moment I was staring at the pile of bin bags on the pavement. They were leaking, a yellowish stream that flowed down the pavement. Pilar was waiting for a reply. In the distance was the sound of a car reversing, but instead of the usual beep beep it was playing a lambada, like a ringtone on an old mobile phone. *What do you mean, no, Pilar?* You can't just do that. You can't not accept an apology. Right? I mean, come on, I'm dying here, my hands are shaking. I didn't just say it for kicks. *For fuck's sake, Pilar, why do you have to make everything so difficult?* The lambada stopped, the car moved away, and Pilar was still waiting for an answer. On top of spitting my apology back in my face, she wanted an answer, an answer I didn't have, that didn't exist. There was no reason. *I don't owe you anything, Pilar, anything.* Except of course I did, I owed her everything. As the bin juice dribbled in the direction of the drain, I shrugged.

'I don't know.'

'That's it?'

I looked at her. She shrugged in imitation.

'You've got nothing else to say for yourself?' she insisted.

I rubbed the blood off my index finger, avoiding her eyes.

'Makes sense,' she went on. 'You always were the thickest kid in class.'

I took a deep breath and felt like the stink of the rubbish was choking me, so much so that I looked down at my shoes expecting the dirty river to have reached me.

'There had to be a reason… What did I ever do to you? Eh? Why? I never did anything to you. Why me?'

Why? Because of so many things. Because of the *Treasure Island* model, because the rest of the class went along with it, because nobody said anything, because it meant no one ever picked a fight with me, because I hated her, just because, because nothing bad ever went on in her house, because she did well at school, because she didn't have any friends, because I wanted to make sure she never had any, because I could.

'Because you were fat.'

As soon as I heard the words on my lips, I closed my eyes. I couldn't keep my mouth shut, so I closed my eyes instead. Shit.

'No, no,' I tried to apologize. 'That wasn't it, that wasn't what I wanted to say, I—'

'Well, your mum was a whore. And nobody made fun of you.'

I looked up. *What did you say, Pilar?* Now I did want to look her in the face. Had she really said that? Pilar, Pilar Villareal, Porky Pili, had finally done what I'd wanted her to do ever since we were at school together: she'd given me a reason.

'What did you say?'

'She was always sleeping around, everyone knows that's why your dad left.'

I felt my nails digging into my palms, my fists closing.

'Even your own mum can't stand you.'

I breathed out hard, like a fighting bull in a film. I looked at her and my legs started trembling, a different kind of tremor, more familiar. 'Breathe, child, breathe,' Aunt Anahí would have said.

'Yep, I was the fat girl,' Pilar went on. 'But at least my mum was never embarrassed to be my mum.'

I took a step up. *Embarrassed? She was embarrassed?*

'You know what, Villareal, I came here to fix things between us but, I'm warning you, you better stop now or...'

'You're warning me?' she interrupted.

'Stop talking about things you know nothing about.'

'But everyone knows. Everyone knows your mum used to say you were her sister, that's why you live with that sicko, that queer uncle of yours.'

Breathe, Melissa, count, Melissa. Imagine you're hitting her, don't move. Fuck breathing, fuck counting, there was nothing to imagine because I already had Pilar up against the wall. I held the front of her jacket in one hand and laid into her with the other. She struggled, writhed, tried to push me off, but I was stronger. I kept going. She scratched me, elbowed me in the face, twice, several times, but I felt nothing. All I felt was heat, like my whole body was on fire. Blood was dripping from her nose, staining her messy locks of hair. Hate. Hate for the past and hate for the present ran like black saliva out of my chest, over my knuckles, onto Pilar's face, where I wanted to leave it forever, so it could never come after me again. Pilar was screaming.

'Help! Get her off me! Get her off me!'

And it was her fear, real fear, like she was being attacked by a rabid animal, that brought me back to earth. I jumped away and ran off down the street, like a stray dog when somebody picks up a stone. *Fucking hell, Pilar, fucking hell. Why do you have to make everything so difficult?*

'See what you made me do?' Dad used to ask, as he picked up pieces of glass in the living room or as Mum cried or before he slammed the door to the flat and disappeared. 'See?'

I hate you, Pilar. I hate you so much.

I ran as fast as I could. My face was throbbing, my head hurt. With each step I came apart a little more. I felt like a car being stripped of one layer of paint after another until all that's left is the crap underneath, the crap that's always been there, that never disappeared, despite all the colour and the polish, the crap's always been there underneath. I'd found her: the old Melissa Noriega, the one I'd never stopped being. When I was far away enough, I touched my left eyelid gingerly. It was swelling up and I couldn't see through it properly. I didn't have to look at myself to know it was bad.

*

I hid my hands inside my jacket sleeves so Mum wouldn't see my knuckles. I sat on the sofa, closed my eyes and waited. Footsteps, and then I felt Mum sit down too. I heard water trickling into the bowl and knew she was wringing out a cloth.

'How exactly did you fall, my love?'

She placed the warm cloth carefully over my left eyelid and applied gentle pressure. The drops of water tickled as they slid down my cheek towards my chin, like borrowed tears.

'I tripped.'

There was a silence, then I cracked open my right eye to see her reaction. *Do you believe me? Do I want you to believe me?* When I looked around, I was disoriented for a second, because I didn't recognize our living room. Then I remembered we were at Adela's.

'Jesus, it's pretty bad, I wonder if we should take you to hospital.' She wrung out another cloth. 'Is it very painful?'

I shook my head. It was true – it was uncomfortable, especially the swelling, and it itched a bit, but it didn't hurt. Or maybe it did, maybe it hurt so much I couldn't feel my face, only the veins beating under my skin. In any case, I didn't want to go to hospital. She removed the cloth, soaked it again and laid it on my eyelid a second time.

'Christ,' she said. 'Maybe a slice of potato will help the swelling go down.'

'Potato?'

'Sabanera potato, the purple ones. Hold this, let me see if Adela's got any.'

I looked around the living room with my right eye. The green velvet sofa had a couple of bare patches on the armrests I hadn't noticed before. The feeling of my finger rubbing against one of them confirmed I wasn't dreaming. It was real. Pilar would be at home, crying on the sofa, while her mum looked for purple potatoes in the kitchen, too. No, her mum was probably one of those people who has a little blue ice pack in the freezer. Maybe they weren't even home, maybe they were on the way to the police, to tell them to come and get me, and maybe that was for the best. I pressed on the cloth. Hard. My eye stung and water dripped down my cheek to my neck, soaking into my top.

Suddenly the table vibrated. I reached out my arm for my phone. My forehead throbbed. It was a message from Zapata. Until I read her name, it hadn't occurred to me that it might be about anything other than Pilar, anything other than Corpus Cristi. But there it was, a message from Zapata, a lifeline, a sign that that world – the world of Zapata and the other girls, of Ofelia Uribe, of La Alborada, of Aunt Anahí – still existed. Aunt Anahí. God, I didn't want to think about Aunt Anahí. What would she say when she found out? What would Mum say? What would Zapata say? What was there to say?

I didn't want to open the message. She was probably texting about something stupid. It didn't matter what, the important thing was that, out there, in some part of Bogotá, Zapata still existed and the Melissa she knew also existed. Right? She had to exist, out there in Zapata's head. What was she doing right now? What was she listening to? Some electro-hornpipe group nobody had heard of yet but would be famous in a couple of months? Portuguese jazz? Old-school bolero? Eighties pop? Who knows? With Zapata you never know. I felt like one of those songs Grandad liked, the ones with a slow guitar and a Chilean guy singing super softly, like he hadn't even realized he was singing out loud, singing so gently that at first you don't realize he's singing about death.

Mum came back with several slices of potato spread out on a little plate like a hand of cards. She smiled at me, and I couldn't help but smile back as she sat down next to me, even though I didn't want to smile. I didn't deserve her smile, I didn't deserve her cloths and warm water, nor her sweet words and concern. I didn't deserve any of it.

She slowly took the cloth off and replaced it with a slice of potato. It was cold. I felt the potato milk run down my skin.

'Don't move or it'll fall off, love. There we go, you stay there, give it ten minutes. At least ten, so the swelling goes right down, till it's not so purple… There. This is what I used to do in the mornings, before going to work.'

I tried to see her but couldn't without the potato slipping off. I heard her swallow drily. I reached out my hand and felt about until I found hers. I held it like she used to hold mine.

'I didn't know a potato worked for this,' I said.

Nor did I know how many times Mum had gone to work with a black eye. Or, rather, having covered up a black eye. As though it weren't enough to have one, she also had to get up God knows how early to slice a potato and leave it ten minutes and then put her make-up on carefully so nobody would see it, because she was ashamed. Mum shouldn't have been ashamed of hers, but I did need to be ashamed of mine.

'Have you thought about what I said last night?' she asked, before pushing back a lock of hair that had stuck to my forehead. 'You remember, right?'

'I wasn't *that* drunk.' I laughed faintly.

I'd spent many a night tossing and turning, imagining her saying something like that to me, imagining it word for word. In my head it was more dramatic, to be sure. *Meli, please, I beg you*, she'd plead with me to go with her, and I'd be a bit hesitant at first but only to make my 'of course I will' taste even sweeter. But right then I didn't know what to say, I genuinely didn't. I was lost. I was a mess.

'It's OK, you don't have to give me an answer right now.'

'Would we live here?' I asked quietly, even though it was only us two. 'Not at Adela's, I mean, in our old neighbourhood.'

'No, well, I don't think so… Depends what I can get, but I doubt it. I'm going to come and look at some flats with Jorge next month, you should come with us.'

'Yeah… I'd like that.'

There he was again. Jorge. He sounded like the kind of guy who wore jumpers and bought whole coffee beans to grind at home. Maybe he was the reason Mum went to mass and had stopped smoking and started dressing like the mums who got up and clapped when the national flag was raised at Ofelia Uribe. He was probably the reason Mum was in Bogotá for the weekend. She must've been crazy about him, if they've been together eight months. She didn't even last a year with my dad, before I brought them back together.

Jorge was probably the opposite of my dad, he probably gave her flowers for no reason, cooked meals out of nowhere and fell asleep watching TV with her. There was a period when Dad started cooking. It was January, I remember, because that Christmas he gave my mum a beautiful necklace. It was a whole big thing. I remember there was clapping, and they kissed in the living room like in the movies and we all thought things were going to be different because Dad had never given her jewellery before. He was going to change, he said, he swore he would. I don't know, I think even he believed it. I can just imagine him in the jewellery shop, pointing at the necklace behind the glass. I can imagine him smiling, asking the woman to gift-wrap it, then making some joke about the price before paying.

I also believed it on the morning I found him in the kitchen before school, scraping eggs off the pan and muttering 'stupid piece of shit'. I was late for school, but I couldn't go without breakfast. It was the first time he'd ever made it. He'd made instant coffee and had even laid the table. The eggs weren't bad, but he was pissed off because Mum ate two mouthfuls then scarpered without saying anything, not even 'thanks'. Dad didn't talk to me for the rest of the morning, and I was late for school. Fuckssake. He never made breakfast again.

Maybe Jorge made Mum orange juice every morning. Maybe Jorge was handsome. I couldn't imagine him handsome, but maybe he was. What if I fell in love with him? Like in one of the black-and-white films I watched with Aunt Anahí where the mum and daughter fall in love with the same man, a skinny guy with a thin little moustache that makes him look like a pilot, only he's not a pilot, he's a herpetologist (hepertologist?), a.k.a. someone who studies snakes or something. One day he shows his girlfriend's daughter the laboratory where he's got a bunch of dissected animals and she falls in love, not because of the animals, because dissecting animals is pretty creepy, but because the guy talks so passionately about his work. And because he's a decent guy, when the daughter tries to seduce him, he says no, because he really loves her mother, but the mother breaks up with him anyway because she says she can't be with him knowing it's breaking her daughter's heart. The problem was that they were three people who loved each other too much (or something like that). In all honesty, I didn't pay much attention to the ending because that was when Aunt Anahí ran a hand through my hair and said: 'Hey kid, will you look after me when I'm old and don't know how to use a mobile phone?'

She'd had a date that night. She'd only just started going out again after breaking up with her boyfriend, Carlos. I never found out why they broke up, but I liked Carlos. He always arrived with little bags of these sweet almonds they sold next door to his office, and he would help my aunt wash up after she'd cooked. Once, my aunt fell asleep while they were watching a film and he covered her with a blanket, which I thought was so lovely I couldn't bear to tell him the blanket belonged to Katya. Anahí and I still laugh about that.

That night, I didn't have to ask how her date had gone because she was home by quarter to eleven, and alone. I suggested we open a bottle of wine and watch films for a while. At first, she said she was tired, but I told her a really good film was about to start on the channel she liked. I knew nothing about the film, really. But I did know it wasn't a good idea to be alone after a bad date. So we ended up in the living room, my head on her shoulder and Katya lying at the other end of the sofa, half asleep. It was almost over when she asked me: 'Hey kid, will you look after me when I'm old and don't know how to use a mobile phone?'

'Yes.' I yawned. 'But you'll have to warn your husband so he doesn't freak out that I'm at your house the whole time.'

'Oh, love…' She said with a half-laugh, before taking a sip from her wine glass.

'Fine, you don't have to marry if you don't want to,' I said, 'I don't know why people get married these days anyway… but you've got to have a wedding. Just imagine!'

I sat up suddenly, so excited at the idea that I almost knocked my glass of wine all over her.

'Okay… no more wine for you, my girl.'

'Why not? You'd wear a beautiful white dress, not one of those ugly fishtail ones, something elegant, with a long veil. And as your maid of honour, I'd throw you a crazy hen party with strippers and mariachis. Or stripper-mariachis! Imagine!'

'So, they take off their clothes while they're singing?'

'No, they arrive naked, so you don't have to pay for the extra time.'

'Their trumpets already out of their cases?'

'Yup, straight down to business, nothing but a thong and a sombrero.'

'Who says you'd be the maid of honour?'

'Who else? Aunt Magdalena?'

'I'm sure she'd be delighted. I'll ask her to lend me her wedding dress, too, for good measure.'

'She'd burn it before she let you anywhere near it,' I laughed. 'Her loss. No naked mariachis for Aunt Magda.'

'There'll be no nudity for me either...' She took another sip of wine. 'I'm going to die alone.'

'So dramatic! What would you say to me, if I said something like that?'

'It's different, kiddo.'

'You'll see...'

'What?'

'That tomorrow or when you least expect it you'll find the hepertologist of your dreams.'

'Herpetologist. Can't he be something else?'

'Like what?'

'I don't know, something that doesn't involve snakes.'

'Fine, a doctor, then. No, not a doctor, too busy... I know! A musician! Yeah, a musician. Just think, you could sing and play the piano together, all romantic. Or a model, or, I know, an actor! Even better. A porn star... no, wait, hang on, you said no snakes.'

'Oh, Melissa...'

'Fine, he can be whatever you want. The important thing is that he doesn't live off your money because that role's already taken, it's mine. And he has to like dogs. And he has to like me too, or at least put up with me. I'm afraid there's no getting rid of me.'

'Not ever, kiddo.'

*

When Mum came back into the living room, she swapped out the slice of potato on my eyelid. She said the swelling had gone down a bit, but that I was going to have a nasty bruise. I asked what Jorge's job was.

'He's an architect.'

'Thank God.'

'Why, kid?'

I didn't say *Well, if he was a herpetologist I might fall in love with him*, because Mum wouldn't understand the joke and might actually start to worry. Obviously, there was nothing to worry about, because if I did fall in love with Jorge – which wasn't going to happen – I wouldn't tell Mum. I wouldn't tell anyone – except maybe Zapata – because I wanted to see Mum happy. In any case, Jorge wasn't my type, he was too old (probably).

'Nothing, an architect sounds cool, that's all.'

'I know, right? It's so nice seeing him work and seeing his models and everything.'

Mum sat down next to me.

'What about you, you're into Business Administration, huh?'

I didn't say anything but felt my cheeks flame like I'd been made to read aloud in an English lesson.

'You kept that quiet, didn't you, love?'

'Yeah, well, I've only just applied, I might not even get in.'

'Of course you will, why wouldn't you?'

I shrugged. *Because I'm not going to graduate, for a start*. I thought of telling her about the printer. I needed her help, but I didn't want to ask for it, I didn't want to pressure her or make her think I only cared about the money I might get out of her.

'It's not really a business, it's a restaurant I'd like to manage,' I said.

'A restaurant? Cool. Though I can't imagine you cooking.'

'No, no, the first thing I'd do is hire a chef. Actually, first an accountant, then a chef.'

She laughed.

'Although,' I went on, 'just so you know, I can hold my own in the kitchen these days.'

'Really?'

'Aunt Anahí taught me.'

'Oh yeah? What kind of thing do you make?'

'Everything. Arroz con pollo, lentils, pork, pasta. I could even make you prawns.'

'Then there's no excuse, start planning what you're going to cook for me.'

We fell silent. I thought about what it would be like to have my own restaurant one day, just a little one, but one that was mine. On opening night I'd reserve a table for Mum and Aunt Anahí. I'd bring Mum pasta or lasagne, and I'd bring Aunt Anahí chicken breast with rice. It might not seem like much to anyone else, but she'd appreciate it, because she'd remember (or I'd remind her) that it was the first dish she taught me how to cook and she'd know I was saying thank you. I wouldn't be able to sit down and eat with them because I'd be running around, supervising the kitchen, taking orders, fixing problems as they came up, but when everyone left, the three of us would stay to polish off a bottle of wine. We'd talk for hours, telling stories about the past that would seem funny because they'd feel far away, like we were talking about other people, and all the things that had happened – that I'd done – wouldn't seem so bad.

'I broke a printer.'

'What?'

No, I hadn't broken a printer; anyone could accidentally break a printer. I smashed a printer.

I sat up straight and took the slice of potato off so I could look at her. *I smashed a printer. And I broke into Doña Nancy's house and stole the silver trays, and I killed the Martínez brothers' cat, and I... I attacked Pilar Villareal while you were at mass.*

'I smashed it. I smashed the school printer and I can't graduate unless I pay for it.'

I felt my swollen eyelid throbbing and looked for a loose cuticle on my thumb, but my hands were damp and I couldn't get a grip on it.

'I wanted to ask you... if, well, if maybe you could help me pay for it? It would be a loan, I swear I'll pay you back, I'm working in a shop. I'll pay you a bit each month, I swear, until I've paid it back in full. Plus interest, even, whatever seems fair to you.'

'OK.'

I looked at her in surprise.

'OK?'

'When do you have to pay for it?'

'Tuesday...'

'Tuesday!' she gave a big sigh and shook her head. 'Oh kiddo, I don't know if by Tuesday I can...'

'It's last minute, I know.'

'I'm sorry.'

'It's OK.'

I shouldn't have asked.

I really shouldn't have asked, I didn't want her to think I'd only wanted to see her because of that, to ask her for money for the printer. For lunch, we walked to a Lindi's round the corner from Adela's house. The place was new, but inside it was the same as every other Lindi's, the same yellow-and-red chequered floor, tables with black plastic chairs, the menu in mustard-coloured lettering on the till and that smell of old oil. I wondered if they still did those skinny fries, that was what made Lindi's better than anywhere else. The secret to good chips isn't the potatoes, Aunt Anahí taught me, it's the salt. You have to be really generous with the salt as soon as the chips are out of the oil, so that it sticks. The longer you wait, the worse they'll be. You can also put pepper or whatever else you want on them, but the important thing is to do it quickly. I ordered a Lindi's burger with cheese and no lettuce, medium chips. Mum ordered the same, but with lettuce.

'Picky as ever,' Mum said as we looked for a table that wasn't too dirty.

'I'm not picky, I do like lettuce, it's just it gets the bread all wet and gross. Careful, there's mayonnaise there.'

'You're just like your grandfather, he would only eat beans if they were in a bandeja paisa. Did I get any on me?'

'Let's see – no. Anyway, you can talk. You like milk and you like coffee but you wouldn't drink milky coffee if someone paid you.'

'Milky coffee is for children and old people.'

That made me laugh and we went on talking about milky coffee until the buzzer announced that our order was ready. Mum stood up to get the tray and when she got back the chips looked exactly like I remembered. It wasn't until she sat down and I tried one that I realized they didn't taste as good. Not bad, but not as good.

'It's been ages since I had a burger,' Mum said. 'It's delicious.'

I just nodded because my mouth was full.

'Have you seen that Spiderman film?' she asked. I swallowed.

'Which one? The new one?'

'The one in the cinemas.'

'No, but I heard it's good.'

'We could go tomorrow… though we might not have time, I'm leaving at midday.'

'Next time, then.'

'Deal. Have you seen anything else good recently?'

'Actually, I haven't been to the cinema for ages,' I said, 'but I started watching this new series.'

'Oh yeah?' she asked, trying to yank open her bag and get something out with one hand. 'What channel?'

'Online. Shall I…?'

'All good, thanks,' she said, pulling out her phone. 'What's it about?'

'It's kind of suspensey, a bit weird. There are these two storylines happening at the same time, one in, like, the sixties and the other in, I dunno, 1800 or something, before electricity, but they happen in the same house.'

'Just let me reply to this quickly, one sec.'

I waited as she typed on her phone.

'Done, sorry. So, in the same house.'

'Yeah, it's this huge house, like in a horror film. So in the sixties, there's this girl who goes to the house to look after her great aunt who she doesn't even know, but she doesn't have any children or anyone else. And the house is full of weird stuff and the great aunt is also super weird, a bit scary.'

'Weird stuff?'

'Yeah, there's a room where the great aunt won't let her touch or change anything and there's a cemetery in the garden and a room full of family portraits but one is covered over with a black cloth and the name's scratched out. Then the other storyline's about the family's past, but it's crazy, it's—'

I stopped because Mum's phone pinged.

'Sorry, give me one sec.'

'Sure.'

'OK... right, go on,' she said as she was texting. 'So, there's all this weird stuff in the house.'

'Yeah, but the craziest part is that, at night, the girl starts seeing this woman wearing old clothes and she's scared because obviously she thinks it's a ghost. But the cool thing, and I'm not spoiling anything because this happens right at the beginning, is that you recognize the woman because she's the protagonist in the other story, the one from the past.'

'OK...'

'And it turns out she's not a ghost, but for some reason, the two time periods kind of come together at night so they can see each other.'

'Hang on, so who was the ghost?' She asked, still looking at her phone.

'No, there aren't any ghosts, they're real people.'

Mum was still texting. I didn't mind people being glued to their phone (unlike Aunt Anahí) but still, I wasn't going to repeat myself every two seconds, so I waited.

'Sorry, sorry, darling, it's Jorge. Give me one second and I'm all yours.'

She stood up with her phone pressed to her ear. *I hope it's nothing serious.* It would have to be serious, right? Otherwise, why would she get up from the table? Maybe they were fighting because they'd hardly seen each other all weekend, because she and I had spent it together. Or maybe it wasn't anything serious, they were planning a surprise. No, that couldn't be it. Maybe the party was cancelled. In the end it couldn't have been anything bad because Mum came back smiling. Still, I asked her, 'All good?'

'Yes, yes, he says hello. So, what were you saying?'

That 'he says hello' stuck with me. I liked knowing she'd talked to Jorge about me, I wanted to know what she'd said, but I couldn't bring myself to ask.

'So, it's a horror series?' asked Mum.

'No, more like a mystery.'

'Good, then I can watch it. Did I tell you I saw a ghost in Mira Plaza?'

'What? What happened?'

'OK, so it was late and we were closing up as usual. And the shop's, like, by this corridor that leads to the toilets. So, yeah, I was there putting stuff away, that kind of thing, when I saw an old woman go down the corridor towards the toilets. And suddenly I hear this scream, a horrible scream, but like, *horrible*, Meli, horrible. I went out to look and there was no one in the corridor or in the bathrooms so I ran back to the shop. And the next day I told Rubén who works with me and he said the place is haunted, that loads of people have seen ghosts there at night. Imagine. I'm never staying late again, nope, not in a million years.'

'Apparently my school's haunted, too. I've never seen anything, but people say that near the gym, round the back, you know where all the food stands are' – as I was talking, I realized Mum had only been to Ofelia Uribe a couple of times and probably didn't remember where they were – 'anyway, the point is, people say that round there there's a construction worker who died when the school was being built.'

'Eek, look,' she said, holding out her arm. 'I've got goosebumps already.'

I smiled. I liked talking about this kind of thing with her, I'd missed it. I'd missed it so much that, for a second, I forgot what had happened that morning with Pilar Villareal. It was only a moment, the time it took to hear her 'Get her off me!' again. You don't have to be a ghost to haunt someone. 'You should be more scared of the living than the dead, love,' Aunt Anahí always said when we watched scary films. I'd say to her, 'Oof, I know, especially the ones who work in banks,' and she'd hit me with a cushion, but she was right. I covered my red knuckles with my other hand.

'Mum?'

'Yeah?'

Do you think people can change?

'Nothing's changed round here, has it?'

'You think so, Meli?'

'Yeah, it's like it's been frozen. Everything's the same.'

'Hmm… I hadn't thought about it, maybe because I feel so different… But now you mention it, everything's pretty much the way we left it, isn't it? What do you think our flat's like now?'

'I guess there's probably another family there… or maybe a couple, or just one person…'

I imagined our flat with the walls painted a light colour, which would make it look bigger. I wondered if whoever lived there looked out of the same window I used to look out of into the street, while wondering if Dad would come back. Maybe they'd hung landscape paintings on the same walls I used to scrape my knuckles on, or even photographs, and in the kitchen where I used to dance salsa with Mum they'd stir soup and fry meat without ever knowing I'd been happy there, at some point.

'If I was a ghost,' I said, 'that's where I'd haunt.'

'The flat?'

'I'd visit Aunt Anahí, but I wouldn't haunt her flat. I'd go round and say hi every now and again, and feed Katya, stroke her, of course. Wash the dishes, once in a while.'

I'd wash the dishes but I wouldn't dry them. Not because I wouldn't have time, because I'd have all the time in the world (I assume), but so she'd know it was me. It would be like leaving a note: 'If I didn't do it when I was alive, I'm hardly going to start now.'

'That's the kind of ghost I need.'

'What about you?'

'What about me?'

'What would you haunt?'

'A spa.'

I laughed.

'You know?' she said, more quietly, like it was a secret. 'We could go and see it, it's not far.'

'The flat?'

No, the spa, Melissa.

'Just to have a nose around.'

Standing in front of the building, my throat all tight and my back sweaty, I imagined taking off my shoe and throwing it at the window. In the air, the shoe would become heavy, heavy like a brick, and bang, it would smash the glass, not just of one window, but all of them, at the same time, like a waterfall. Then we'd run inside, up those narrow stairs that seemed to get longer whenever we had to carry the shopping up them or run away from Dad. I'd knock down the door, the big fat wooden door that Mum used to put a bar across at night and which shook whenever Dad kicked it in the mornings, shouting to be let in. Miracle he never broke it down. I'd break it down, though. I'd fling myself at it with all my strength and the tired door would let me in. I'd cross the living room and go into the room where the crying was coming from. I'd get Mum out first, I'd take her hand and drag her out of the room. Then I'd go back for me, for the stupid little girl scraping her knuckles on the wall. I'd take their hands and drag them out of there as though the flat was on fire and I'd promise: 'Never again.' Just that, 'Never again.' The broken glass would be mixed with the ashes of what had been the bedroom and living room and kitchen. Never, ever again.

I saw it all so clearly, I was surprised there was no smoke coming out of the windows, that the glass was intact, that Mum and I were standing there on the pavement. From the street all we could see was the curtains. They were different to ours.

'I almost bought a gun.'

I looked at Mum, as though to check it had really been her who'd spoken.

'A gun?'

'Thank God I didn't.'

We were silent for a bit. I looked at the building again. It looked small. Tiny even, almost fragile, like a bigger building could gobble it up in a single bite or like a strong wind might take it at any moment. But the things that had happened in there weren't small or fragile. If I'd gone in, maybe the flat would have felt immense to me, like an ocean, with no beginning or end, because the things that happened in there were still happening to me and would maybe never stop. I felt something irritating on my face and when I swiped at my cheek it hurt. I remembered it was swollen. Then I remembered why.

'Do you think...?' I started, then stopped, scared to get too close to the black hole, but I needed to know. 'Do you think we're similar... him and...?'

'No,' Mum replied, before I'd finished asking.

She sounded convinced. There was so much, *so much* that pointed to us being similar, but she hadn't hesitated for even a second. Maybe that was enough. I wanted the fact that she believed it to be enough to make it true. But it wasn't, not until she knew.

'I didn't fall over this morning.'

We were both looking at the building, luckily, that way I didn't have to see her face. My lip started trembling. I took a deep breath and clenched my fists.

'A fight?'

'Yeah.'

'I guessed as much.'

'I'm sorry.'

'I'm not the one you need to say it to.'

But I couldn't say it to Pilar, that much was crystal clear. It hadn't been a fight either, not really – you need two people for a fight. I wanted to say, Mum, it's been years since I've done something like that, it's this neighbourhood, please don't disappear again for another seven months.

'I didn't mean to…'

'I know,' she replied with a sigh. 'Come on, I think it's going to rain.'

We started walking. Part of me felt like the building would stop existing as soon as we left, like in a horror film when the survivors leave the haunted house and when they turn around, the fog parts a little and they realize there's nothing there anymore. I didn't look back, I just held on to that image of the fog, and the building gone forever.

'I'm glad you told me,' Mum said.

'Do you still want me to go to the party tonight?'

'Of course, darling, I want you to meet Jorge.' Then she paused for a moment. 'But maybe best not say anything about the fight, OK?'

'Course.'

She paused again, like she was about to say something else, something important. I looked at her, but in the end, she said nothing. Maybe it was better that way. Maybe I wouldn't have liked what she was going to say anyway.

SUNDAY AFTERNOON

As I said, I heard once that the body can only feel one kind of pain at a time. That Sunday I started suspecting it wasn't true. For starters, I'd woken up with a headache, thanks to the Bacardi and passionfruit cocktails, but by the afternoon I felt like I'd been tied to a motorbike and dragged ten blocks. Everything hurt, inside and out, an astonishing collection of muscular aches, scratches and bruises. Or who knows, maybe it's true what they say, maybe these weren't separate kinds of pains but rather one single pain, so big and powerful it had spread around my entire body, from my head to my toes, as though looking for a way out.

Mum had gone out for a wander, and I'd stayed at Adela's. 'Have a little snooze,' Mum had said. She was always so optimistic with her snoozes, as though having one was the easiest thing in the world. I battled with Adela's TV for a while, before giving up and deciding to go to the pharmacy for some kind of painkiller. For that, and to stop myself thinking, thinking, thinking about Pilar, the building, the party, everything.

I don't like crying. OK, I'm pretty sure no one likes it, though it's not like I've done a survey. But I really hate it. I'm not sure when I started doing it, but to stop myself crying I used to punch the wall. Not hard. Gently, rhythmically, mechanically, like a drum or a machine. Yeah, slow and steady, until my knuckles started kind of buzzing and went all green and swollen, like rotten potatoes. But it was OK, because I could concentrate on it, on the buzzing, the pins and needles, concentrate until the shouting coming from the other room disappeared (replacing one pain with another). Afterwards my knuckles would throb and the flat would fall silent again. But it stopped me from crying. Dad never said 'cry'. He'd say: 'Here we go, mewling again,' or 'You gonna start mewling? Enough of your mewling!' Mewling sounded worse. Mewling is what kittens do when they're kicked or abandoned, mewling is for animals, it's what people do when they don't feel like people. And sometimes it really sounded like that, through the wall. I still hate crying. Because when the tears start to fall and my nose gets snotty and my face is all hot, I can still hear the insults and the yelling from the room next door. The tears fall, gross, salty, hot, and once again I'm shut up in my room. Alone in my room, wanting someone to come and get me out or grab my hand and tell me it'll be over soon, that everything will be OK. Alone in my room and hating myself for not going out and doing something because Mum is crying, she's mewling on the other side of the wall and I'm in here alone, punching the wall instead of doing something. Like what? Anything, just something to make it stop. I hate crying.

I asked someone where the nearest pharmacy was. It felt strange to have to ask for directions in Corpus Cristi. It also felt strange to walk around not knowing if people recognized me, or were staring because I had a black eye, or if they recognized me because I had a black eye. Eyes, eyes, eyes. But when I was about to go into the pharmacy it was me who stared. I stood there. *Can it be?* I peered in just long enough to see if it really was Víctor inside.

Karen was right, he'd gained a few pounds but they kind of suited him. He was letting his beard grow, his hair was shorter, almost shaved at the sides, and his back was very broad. Part of me had still imagined him as a thirteen-year-old whose palms sweated whenever we walked holding hands. My first ex, my first boyfriend, my first shag… did I want to say hello? What if he didn't remember me? *No, I was his first everything, too.* What was I going to say?

When I was eight, I made up that I'd been born without tear ducts, or without tears, or with some strange disease; the point was, I told people I was physically unable to cry. And everyone was concerned and asked questions that I answered in so much detail I could have written a manual on the subject, and everyone was amazed, except for Víctor. Víctor didn't buy it. 'Oh yeah?' he said. 'Yes.' 'Well, I don't believe it.' 'Don't believe me then.' 'Chop an onion and we'll watch.' 'Fine, I will.'

I thought that would be the end of it, but two days later the little upstart shows up with a giant fucking onion in his schoolbag. 'Shame you didn't bring anything to cut it with, idiot.' 'Chill, Ardila has a knife.' A teeny knife that wouldn't even cut through butter, but whatever, he borrowed it all the same. So I started chopping the onion. More classmates had arrived by this point. I was trying to get through the first layer, the juice was running and spitting, and I could feel my eyes burning. Then: 'What's going on here, may I ask?' It was like someone had turned on the Bat-Signal – the head of year appeared, frowning, hands on hips. All three of us got a telling-off. Ardila for having a knife, me for using it, and Víctor... for organizing the whole thing, I guess, or maybe for bringing an onion into school. I guess she assumed Víctor had a) stolen it, or b) lied to his Mum so he could bring it, saying it was for a class activity or something. It didn't occur to her that c) Víctor might have bought it himself with the change from his lunch money. It wasn't exactly a luxury item. Anyway, I spent the afternoon in detention. But at least my dignity was saved.

Years later, once we were a couple, Víctor said he'd done it to get my attention. I guess it worked, because he ended up being my first boyfriend. Real boyfriend, I mean. Technically, Sergio was first, he lasted a week, and then there was Mateo, who lasted a lunch break. But Víctor I actually liked. That's why it hurt so much when he came to me one morning at school with tears in his eyes to tell me his dad had been in an accident. My first impulse was to say, 'Stop mewling, being a pussy's not going to fix anything,' but I didn't, because I knew I'd regret it if I did. So I said nothing. I looked at him, then turned around and left. He was crying, and I left. I didn't say anything. *Anything*. His dad in the hospital and not even an 'I'm sorry'. I think if he hadn't been too busy worrying about his dad, he would have broken up with me there and then, with good reason. I turned my fucking back on him.

But turning my back on him was better than saying something that would hurt him. If I'd stayed, I would have hurt him, berated him for crying. And not just that. I turned my back on him because I didn't want to look at him anymore. I didn't want to see Víctor crying because when he told me his dad had been in an accident, I wondered what I would have done if my dad was in the hospital. I couldn't do what Víctor had done, because it was my dad who taught me not to mewl, to be strong. But I didn't know if I'd be physically able, anyway – if I'd even feel like crying for him, I mean. I suspected I wouldn't, and that worried me. It was one thing to want to cry and not do it (brave) and another thing entirely not to feel like crying at all (deficient). What would that mean? You're supposed to love your parents, or at least try to. Who wouldn't feel like crying when they saw their dad seriously injured in the hospital? Was there something wrong with me after all? Not physically, not with my eyes or tear ducts, but wrong inside, deep down, where the doctors couldn't get in to fix me.

I didn't like any of that, so I turned my back and decided not to think about it anymore. Why? It didn't matter whether I cried or not, my dad wasn't around these days, he'd become the black hole, the one that conversations couldn't get too close to because it would swallow them up and end them. And still, there was part of me that was a bit jealous. Víctor could cry over his dad without needing to think about it. He just could and that was that.

It was hard not to like Víctor's dad. Always laughing at his own jokes, always with a bit of local gossip to share. But the thing I didn't like about Víctor's parents when we were at school was that I didn't recognize the person I became around them. It was the same with Karen's mum.

Whenever I was invited over for a meal, I'd put my fork in my left hand like Aunt Anahí taught me, wait before starting, take my plate into the kitchen, and once, once I even did the washing up and everything. Me, who at that time wouldn't wash up a thing in my own home. But table etiquette was the least of it – the main problem was when we talked. Because when we talked, I'd forget they were Víctor's parents and not my own.

Sometimes I felt like ratting on Víctor just to please them. Like I could tell them he was a smoker now or that the time he arrived home all scraped up wasn't because he'd been hit by a cyclist but because he got into a fight with a Santa Fe fan outside the stadium. They cared about those kinds of things, and if it was me who told them, God, they'd be so grateful. Awful. I didn't do it, but I felt like I could.

What I did do was reply to everything with 'señor' and 'señora', never a 'What?' or a swear word. I never restrained myself like that, not even with Mum, not even with Aunt Anahí. I said thank you to everything and made an effort to remember what they'd told me last time: whether his grandmother was ill, or one of the machines at the garage was broken, so I could ask them how the grandmother/machine was doing next time around.

I always got the impression his mum didn't like me as much as his dad did. Maybe because I was her son's first girlfriend (strike one). Or maybe because I liked talking to her husband (strike two). Or maybe she just pretty much had the measure of me (out). Whatever it was, it meant that every time she argued with Víctor I took her side. Obviously, this annoyed Víctor, but that paled in comparison to the thrill I felt at the 'See?' from his mum when she agreed with me (after I'd agreed with her).

It was easier with Karen's mum, she'd liked me from the start. I think it was because Karen was all quiet and shy – well, at first, because once she found her confidence, heaven help us all. She was more solitary when we were little, but after Dayana and I adopted her, her mum relaxed because she knew she'd always have someone to hang out with at lunch. Sometimes, when I went to her house, her mum came into her room with biscuits and fizzy drinks, sat on the bed and ended up telling us about her classes at the Libre, about the teacher who started shouting that he was having a heart attack and asked them to call an ambulance, but it turned out to be trapped wind, or her first day of work when she was running for the lift carrying a bunch of folders, shouting for someone to hold it for her, when she tripped on the 'Wet Floor' sign. 'The papers flew everywhere,' she laughed, 'and I went down while everyone in the lift looked on.' These were stories I'd heard so many times I knew them by heart.

Karen was a bit embarrassed that her mum always told the same stories, but eventually she realized that not only did I not mind, I actually liked it. Karen always realized these things without my needing to say them, not like Dayana and me. When I didn't want to be at home, I always called Karen first. 'Can we hang out?' I didn't need to say anything more, she understood the rest.

When I went into the pharmacy, Víctor was leaning on the counter with his back to me. I hesitated a moment before tapping him twice on the shoulder. He apologized, thinking he was in the way, and made space beside the till, before looking at me properly. When he smiled, I knew he'd recognized me. I smiled back.

'I can't believe it,' he said.

'Víctor Víctorino Pinzón.'

'La Noriega.'

He hugged me, smelling of hair oil and spray deodorant. What must I smell of?

'What are you doing here?'

'How are you?'

We spoke at almost the same time, then laughed.

'To what do we owe the pleasure?'

'I'm visiting my mum. Well, she's visiting and we came to spend the weekend. You? What's new?'

'Me, I'm good, working in the garage. What happened?'

He pointed to my eye before turning to the shopkeeper, who had left a couple of boxes on the counter.

'The Martínez brothers gave me a welcome back present,' I answered, and pointed to the boxes to change the subject. 'What's all this?'

'For my dad. Thanks, man.'

'His back's still bad?'

'Yeah, there's no changing that now, Noriega. He had to stop working so much, the garage was killing him. You know, he asks about you sometimes. He always remembers that you took him packets of crisps when he was in the hospital.'

I smiled.

'I'd forgotten that.'

'Whenever he asks, I always think "I'll text Noriega", but you know how it is, you get caught up in other things, and, well… I'm glad I can finally tell him now.'

'Say hello from me. And how's your mum? Your brothers?'

'Well, Mum's knackered because Germán's hit puberty and become an absolute nightmare. No one can stand him.'

'No! Little Germán? I still remember him in his first communion outfit, with his hair all full of gel.'

'Ha. Yeah, that's ancient history now.'

The shopkeeper cleared his throat as though to remind us we were supposed to pay and get out of there. I asked for some painkillers.

'Your eye?' asked Víctor.

I nodded.

'They really went for it. But knowing you, I can only imagine how they ended up.'

The joke touched a nerve. I don't know if he noticed, but either way, I changed the subject.

'And how's the garage?'

'It's hard, I guess, because I'm also taking classes at community college.'

'Really?'

'Yeah, gonna see if I can expand, so my dad doesn't have to work anymore.'

'Víctorino! I'm so glad you're studying.'

The shopkeeper started giving me options. I wasn't paying attention and just asked for the strongest thing he had.

'Well, I'm only just starting out,' Víctor went on, 'but you know, little by little. What about you?'

'I work part-time in a shop, but mainly I'm studying. You know me, always got my nose in a book.'

He laughed.

'Books about perreo, right.'

The man asked me how many pills I wanted, and I realized I wasn't sure how much money I had with me.

'Sometimes, yeah, but I'm about to graduate. Just one, please.'

'That's great, that's great. And are you still living with your uncle… your aunt?'

'Yeah, I live with my aunt here in Bogotá.'

'Here you go, señorita.'

'Put it on my account, mate,' said Víctor, as I was pulling out my wallet.

'No, Víctorino, you don't have to do that.'

'Don't worry, when you're rich and powerful I'll make sure you return the favour.'

I thanked him and the shopkeeper.

'You should have said so before, I'd have bought the whole packet,' I teased, as we headed out into the street.

'That's exactly why I didn't. Anyway. Any boyfriends? I've got to get all the gossip for my dad.'

'Tell him yes, but only a few.'

He laughed. I liked knowing I could still make him laugh so easily.

'I don't believe you, Noriega.'

'I told you, I'm all about the hard work these days. You?'

'I've been seeing this girl from college for a month or so. See how long she puts up with me.'

I smiled. I wondered how long we would have lasted if I hadn't left town. We wouldn't still be together, I figured, five years was too long. I also figured it was better that way, because sooner or later we'd have ended up hurting each other. I was glad I left before that happened.

'I bumped into Karen the other day,' he said. 'But we didn't really have a chance to talk. She seems kinda lost. I can see why… Did you know…?'

'Yeah, I talked to her yesterday.'

'Complicated.'

'Very. You don't…?'

'Kids? No! Well, not that I know about…'

'There could be five little Víctorinos running around out there.'

'Terrifying thought.'

'No country could handle that.'

He pulled a pack of cigarettes out of his trouser pocket. Meanwhile, I swallowed the pill. Neither of us had any intention of saying goodbye just yet.

'Yeah, God help me,' he said. 'I mean, obviously, if it happened – want one? – then I'd just get on with it.'

'No, thanks. Better for it not to happen.'

'Amen.'

'I hope Karen's all right,' I concluded. 'That she's happy.'

Or, if she isn't, that she figures it out quickly.

A metallic noise made me jump and almost slam into Víctor. I quickly moved away. I was nervous, I didn't want him to think I still liked him. I realized I hadn't said anything when he'd told me about his girlfriend.

'It must be the construction site up there,' he said.

'What are they building?'

'A sports centre, a big one. Looks like it's gonna be really ugly though.'

'A sports centre? Here?'

'See for yourself, Melissa María.'

'Who'd have believed it. Not the bit about it being ugly, that anyone could believe.'

'Things are changing round here. It's more chill… I mean, it's not exactly safe, but it's nothing like before. You've still got to be careful at night. Although, if that's anything to judge by,' he said, pointing at my face, 'maybe during the day too. What happened with the Martínez brothers anyway?'

'They shoved me against a fence.'

'Did they say anything?'

'Nothing. I dunno, they just ran off.'

'And it was definitely them? Because people still get mugged round here all the time, about a month ago Germán had his headphones nicked in the middle of the day.'

'They didn't take my phone.'

'Maybe they got scared. They realized it was you and said, nope, better not get on the wrong side of her.'

'Yeah, it was probably that, they saw my muscles and bam, off they ran. Anyway, I'm glad I've still got my phone. And it was definitely them. But I can't really complain, I had it coming.'

He looked at me, confused.

'You don't remember?' I asked.

'Oh! The cat? What happened again? It got sick or something, right?'

'It died.'

'It died?'

'Now we're even, I guess. And… I probably deserve a thump from you, too.'

'I've never had a cat.'

'Thank God, or I'd have killed it by now. No, because… remember after your dad's accident? You came to school all cut up, crying and everything, and told me about it and I just stood there like an idiot, then left without saying anything at all.'

'I don't remember.'

'It was before classes started, the morning after the accident. You were so upset…'

'I don't remember crying at school.'

I looked at him. Back then I would have known whether he was lying.

'Anyway, the point is I was a piece of shit and I wanted to say I'm sorry.'

'Well, thanks Noriega, but in that case, I owe you, like, a thousand apologies. I was an imbecile. Still am, but a bit less now. I mean, we were what, thirteen, fourteen? I didn't lose too much sleep over it.'

'Even so.'

'Even so, no one should be going around punching you in the face, doesn't matter how dead their cat is.' He chucked the cigarette butt away and let the smoke stream out through his nose. 'If we run into the Martínez brothers I'll return the favour.'

I laughed and looked at him to see if there was a trace of seriousness behind that promise. I wondered how I would feel if he actually did. I'd say no, try to hold him back, maybe, but honestly, deep down I'd be a teeny bit pleased. It would be like the time at that steak place, De la Parrilla a la Mesa (or was it Parrilla y Carbón? Parrilla y Sazón? Sabor y Parrillón?).

I was with Aunt Anahí and Mum, who at the time was still living with us. I remember it as one of those super rare days when all three of us were in a good mood. The food looked delicious, there was a whole long list of side dishes, Andean potatoes, roasted plantain, even salads (though who orders a salad in a Parrilla y Carbón?), and you could choose up to three for no extra cost. Then the waiter came. That fucking waiter.

'May I take your order? What can I get you, señor?'

Señor. At first, I thought I'd misheard, but the dickhead made sure he ended every single phrase with 'señor' this and 'señor' that. It wasn't an honest mistake, because by this time, there was no room for confusion. If the waiter had needed to sit someone at the next table and had said, 'The table there, next to the gentleman in blue,' the customer wouldn't have known where to sit. He'd have had to say, 'Sit there, next to the lady in blue.' The shitty waiter just said it to fuck with Aunt Anahí. And it worked. She tried to ignore him, but she had completely deflated – with Anahí you can always tell because her hands get fidgety and she goes very quiet. That day she didn't complain, she just took sip after sip of her drink, kept sipping even when there was only ice left. Mum asked to speak to the manager, before my aunt could protest, and said, 'We want a different waiter.' And the motherfucker just looked at us and replied, 'You'd be better off finding a different restaurant.' I was a little weasel back then, so I waited till the waiter came past holding a bunch of trays and stuff (I really was a weasel) and stuck out my foot. He fell hard, face first, onto the floor. Plates broke, cutlery went flying, the floor was a sea of rice, bits of ceramic and spare ribs.

'Oof, careful, señor,' I said, holding out my hand to help him up. 'You should get some glasses to help you see properly.'

He refused my hand and went off, faking a limp, to look for a dustpan and brush. It wasn't such a bad fall – I'm sure what hurt most was his dignity.

'Melissa!' Aunt Anahí scolded me.

'What?'

'What do you mean, "What?" What were you thinking? You can't go round hurting people.'

I looked at Mum, hoping she'd back me up. She just nodded. I sighed.

'OK, but… didn't it feel just a little bit good? A teensy bit? Don't tell me it didn't feel a teensy bit good.'

Aunt Anahí looked at me and gave a half-smile.

'A teensy bit… just, don't even think about doing something like that again, you hear me?'

That's what I'd feel like if Víctor smashed the Martínez brothers' faces in. It would be a bit scary to see him like that, fists clenched, his face red and contorted with anger, the face of a man rather than a child. And I'd run over and say enough, stop, and I'd try to pull him away, but I might quite enjoy seeing him do that for me, though I wouldn't admit it to anyone.

Yeah, I'd have enjoyed it, because it would mean he still cared about me, but also because I'd have liked to see a little bit of the old Víctor. Just a glimpse of him, underneath the Víctor who looked after his family and took classes at the community college, the old Víctor who got into fights outside the stadium at the weekend. Maybe I'd have liked to see him do that because I still fancied him a teensy bit. But which Víctor? The old one or the new? Or both? I fancied the person he'd become, but maybe because I knew the person he'd been.

'I don't know, Víctorino, I think we'd better leave the Martínez brothers in one piece.'

'You don't think I can take them?'

'There's two of them, only one of you, and they're pretty hench these days.'

'And I'm not?'

'I mean…'

He looked at me, feigning indignation. If times had been different, he'd have started to tickle me.

'And I'm not, Melissa María?'

'You have other qualities.'

'Let's leave it at that.'

'I never asked: why "María"?'

'Because you needed a second name. That's why you were always a hopeless case. You can't tell someone off properly without a second name.'

'No, you already explained that part. I mean, why, of all the names in the world, would you choose María?'

'What's wrong with María?'

'There are more Marías in the world than non-Marías.

I don't know, Víctorino, you could have been more creative, that's all.'

'I think it suits you.'

Then I just smiled and shook my head, thinking maybe he was right. Not about the María part – it absolutely did not suit me – but that I needed a second name. If I had one, I'd use it, not because I didn't like Melissa, but so I could start over again, be someone else, someone who did things properly.

'Remember the time you brought an onion into school, Víctorino?'

'Ah, the things we do for love.'

'If you'd brought flowers, like a normal person, we'd have all saved ourselves a detention.'

'If I'd brought flowers, you'd have thrown them back in my face, Noriega.'

We laughed, because we both knew it was true.

'Seriously, though, why did you make that up?' he asked. 'That you couldn't cry?'

'Who says I made it up?'

'I guess I'll never know, you never did manage to slice that onion... But no, I lie, I have seen you cry.'

'When?'

'When you broke your hand.'

'Thumb.'

'At Dayana's party.'

'Let's not talk about that night.'

I meant it as a suggestion, but it came out as an order. We were silent for a moment.

'I only ever saw you cry that day,' I said. 'That morning at school.'

'That was because I'd had zero sleep after the accident, and we didn't know if the old man was going to make it or not. We got a proper fright.'

I wanted to say that he didn't have to explain, that it was OK, but I couldn't find the words. *I wish I could cry like that for my dad, Víctorino.* It was getting dark, I ought to be heading back. When we said goodbye, he said next time I was in town I should come to his place for lunch. It sounded like he meant it, and I realized I really would like to do that, that maybe I could even come back to the neighbourhood just for that. After we gave each other a hug and a kiss goodbye, I took a couple of steps before I stopped and turned.

'Víctorino?'

'Noriega?'

I'm happy for you.

'You better invite me to your graduation.'

I turned around and walked on without waiting for a reply.

'Right back atcha!'

I laughed, and kept walking.

I took the same route back, but this time, walking in the other direction, I came face to face with a huge mural I hadn't seen before, on the side of a building. This was nothing like the graffiti on the other walls: this could have been in a gallery. But it wasn't in a gallery, it was there, in our neighbourhood, and that was worth so much more. I stopped to look at it.

It was of a man on his knees on a beach, washed up from a shipwreck. Behind him, you could see the sea and the boat going down. The man's clothes were in tatters and he was holding out his hands, palms open, fingers stretched, a trickle of sand running through them. He was looking ahead of him, at me, and it occurred to me that he was Pilar, Pilar Villareal, as though she'd been trapped inside her *Treasure Island* model when I destroyed it. That's why the man was looking at me like that, exhausted.

'Why me?'

I don't know, Pilar, it was never about you.

Pilar used to cry a lot, but hardly ever at school (she knew I'd never have let her forget it). But she'd turn up for lessons with her eyes swollen and dark rings under them.

I made you think it was all about you. About what you did or didn't do, what you said, what you wore, how you looked. The truth was, none of that ever mattered.

One time she did cry in the playground, sitting at a table by herself.

Even if you'd changed everything, taken yourself apart and put yourself back together again with completely different parts, you wouldn't have escaped.

No one went over to ask if she was OK.

It was because I needed something I thought you had.

Nor did anyone ask what had happened, why she was crying. Everyone knew the answer.

It was never about you.

I felt my cheeks flame and my throat constrict. I left before my eyes began to fill. I walked quickly, not looking back. I fled.

I hate crying.

SUNDAY NIGHT

At first, I didn't let the song distract me. I concentrated on my make-up, on getting the eyeshadow to sit so no one would guess it was hiding a black eye. With every stroke of the brush it seemed less likely that there was a bloody mess right there under the skin. I thought how weird it was that you could see the blood like that, as if the skin was just a bit of translucent paper, like those napkins people use to dry buñuelos fresh out of the deep-fat fryer. I pressed down with the brush hard enough for it to hurt, on purpose, to prove that it was real, that it wasn't just a mark.

The song was still playing – it had these really weird bells. I tried not to pay attention to it, because if I did, my mind would wander far far away, and I needed to stay anchored there, in Adela's flat, concentrating on getting ready for Jorge's party. I had to make sure I impressed Mum's boyfriend enough that he'd never even imagine what I'd done that morning. But the song kept breaking into my consciousness as it built up to the chorus. Zapata had ruined me. It was her fault I could no longer listen to music in peace.

*

'I dunno, Zapatico, it sounds like the kind of music they play in lifts.'

The two of us were sitting in her room, with her laptop open on the bed. She always used the computer, even though she had these amazing imported speakers. That day she was playing me a tango-bolero mix, but Italian.

'Lift music! God, give me patience, because if you give me strength, I'll kill her. Listen properly, Norieguis. It's so… it's sad, but happy at the same time, it's got that nostalgia… it's like… You know what? Just listen again.'

Without waiting for a reply, she played the song again from the beginning.

'Listen properly. Imagine this: two people were each other's first love, but life got in the way and they didn't end up together, even though they were in love. Then they meet again years later. They're both married to other people but they decide to have one last dance, for old times' sake. And as they dance, they realize they still love each other as much as before, that's the happy bit, but that thing you can hear underneath, that violin, that's the sad bit.'

'Because they aren't happy with the people they married?'

'No, they are, that's the worst part. They love other people but don't want to let each other go, that's why they don't want the song to end even though they know it has to. See?'

I gave her a mocking smile. I understood completely – I could feel all those things in the song, but I always liked to pretend I didn't agree. I shook my head.

'All this madness of yours'll be wasted on a law firm.'

'I know, right?'

She said it with a kind of half-smile that made me suspect that maybe she'd applied to study music or art or something, only she hadn't told me yet.

'I've got a business idea for you,' she went on. 'Let's open a music restaurant.'

'Like with live music?'

'Not just live music! You can get that in any old dive. So, we divide it into sections. Each section's a different kind of music, and everything in that section has to do with that kind of music – the decorations, obviously, but also the food. It has to taste like the songs, know what I mean?'

'Yeah, but I don't like that it's divided by genre. We should have themed seasons instead, you know? Like when you switch radio stations. So one month we'll have one kind of music and the next another, etc.'

'See?'

'What?'

'You have good ideas, when you actually try.'

I punched her softly on the arm and we laughed.

Mum and I were still getting ready to go out to Jorge's, but the song had hit the chorus and I couldn't ignore it any longer. I'd never heard it before but it reminded me of Aunt Magdalena's house, of being in her living room, with her caramel sofas, pushed a bit too close together to make way for the nativity scene. For me, Aunt Magda's house was always decorated for Christmas, like it was in a snow globe, because even before she fell out with her sisters we only ever visited during novenas. This song wasn't a Christmas song, but it had bells and a high-pitched voice that could have been a woman's or a child's, so it sounded like it might be a Christmas carol, except it was about a lost love instead of the baby Jesus.

I never heard that song at Magdalena's house, but still it reminded me of her living room and her telling me and my cousins off for playing with the little figures in the nativity scene. It was a false memory. And because it was a false memory, I could see Mum with my aunts, both of them, turning a natilla mould over onto a tray. They were laughing because half of it had got stuck in the mould and their laughter was like the trumpet in the background of the song. The doorbell rang, it was Alfredo's family, and when Aunt Magda went to let them in, Aunt Anahí went with her, and Magda put a hand on her shoulder and said: 'This is my sister.' And they both smiled because it was the first time Aunt Magdalena had said that, and the voice stopped singing but the bells repeated the melody until it slowly faded.

'Do you know what this song's called?' I asked, but Mum didn't hear because she was concentrating on her make-up.

Then I thought that the next time I heard it, it would remind me of two places, the false memory of Aunt Magdalena's house and that moment in Adela's flat, getting ready for Jorge's party. I'd tell Zapata this when I saw her on Tuesday. Tuesday felt so far away, a dot on the horizon, far off but still real, a refuge, hope. Hope of leaving our old neighbourhood behind and especially of leaving the old Melissa behind, leaving her locked up and throwing away the key, going back to being Melissa from La Alborada, from Ofelia, the real Melissa. Because that was the real

Melissa, right? The one who fell silent in history lessons and couldn't handle the infinite answers in calculus, who played basketball like a regular student and who was going to graduate, that was the real Melissa. It had to be, because it couldn't be the other one, the one who had punched Pilar Villareal in the face.

'Is it even?' Mum asked, opening her eyes really wide so I could see the black line she'd just drawn.

I looked. She was even doing her make-up differently these days. She used to use more eyeliner, more colour – now it looked like she was going to the office on a Monday morning, not to a party. She didn't look bad, just more boring. I said yes, it was even.

'How are you getting on?'

'I'm nearly done. What do you think?'

She looked at me. I batted my eyelashes and smiled, but she was quiet.

'That bad?'

'What? No, no! It's just – when did you get so grown-up?'

Something about the way she said it, semi-distracted, semi-eager, made me suspect that, no, that wasn't what she'd been thinking. Mum had been distracted, sometimes asking me the same thing several times, her eyes semi out of focus, like she was looking in the mirror but without seeing herself reflected there. Maybe she was worried about the fight, because I was going to meet Jorge, or, rather, he was going to meet me. Despite the make-up and the potato slices, my face was still swollen and my eyelid a bit dark. If anyone asked, we'd agreed to say I'd been elbowed during a basketball game on Friday, which was something that really happened to Zapata once. It was a good lie because it was a true story, we'd just borrowed it. I hardly had to invent anything.

Outside it had started to rain. Why does it always rain when you're about to go out? It started as a drizzle but within a couple of minutes it had got heavy and we couldn't figure out how best to get there. Adela had taken the car to work and there was no way we could walk to the bus stop without getting drenched. Mum started to look distressed, pacing up and down, looking at her phone as she tried to get hold of a taxi. I'd downloaded a new app onto my phone that almost always worked, though I'd never tried it out in Corpus Cristi.

'Unbelievable. Can't even get a taxi in Bogotá these days,' Mum complained.

It was still early, only ten past eight, but she'd been jumpy ever since we started getting ready. I was jumpy too, but less so. We both knew that, more than a party, tonight was a test. Like a rehearsal but also an exam. A rehearsal of the three of us in the same place and an exam for me, to see if I could manage to get Jorge to like me. Pass or fail. It was important, very, because I knew Mum wouldn't bother introducing me to Jorge if it wasn't serious, and if it was serious, then we had to get on well. Or at least pretend to. It shouldn't be hard, because Jorge sounded like a decent guy and I – well, I could be charming. It wasn't like I was shy. That had never been the problem.

Of course Mum was nervous. She would have had every right to be before, but there's no need now. That was then, because back then I was... the way I was.

And for a moment I believed it, but only for the time it took to look in the bathroom mirror and see my dark eyelid, the bruise there, under the make-up, the Pilar bruise, the bruise Pilar had to give me after I shoved her against the wall and hit her as she shouted, 'Get her off me! Get her off me!' *Get her off me too, get that off me.* It was this neighbourhood. The La Alborada me, the Zapata me, the me who cooked with Aunt Anahí and swept Señor Héctor's shop, that was the me who would meet Jorge. My phone vibrated. I looked at the screen.

'There's a car on its way.'

'Oh, good! Thanks, love.'

She kissed my forehead, careful not to leave a lipstick mark. I smiled. I liked that, making her feel like she didn't have to worry, and I wondered if I'd feel like crying the next morning when she kissed my forehead again before leaving for Bucaramanga.

The car, a red Mazda, smelled like dog shampoo. It wasn't a bad smell, it reminded me of bathing Katya, stroking her while I lathered up her legs and tummy. Katya hated baths, but she loved being dried afterwards with the hairdryer, on low because if it was too high she'd start barking and run off. What was Katya doing right now? Sleeping, probably. I thought about how it would break my heart if I got home one day and she didn't recognize me, and that it would break her heart if one day I didn't come home at all, if I no longer lived with her.

Outside it was still raining, but it feels different watching the rain from inside a car. Bogotá is so pretty when it rains at night. It always looks prettier at night (because you can see less) but when it's raining the lights reflect off the asphalt and the puddles and the drops that slowly get fatter and fatter until they run down the window. Since Mum knew the way and I didn't, she sat in the front. It was good, that way she made conversation with the driver and I watched the rain.

I didn't feel like I was on my way to a party. Mum was wearing a beautiful white blouse with a delicate bow at the front and a light-blue coat, very elegant. It was funny to think of that beautiful top hiding her Tweety tattoo. Had Jorge seen it? Probably, it wasn't that easy to hide. I wondered what he said the first time he saw it. If they'd laughed. If he'd asked about Mum's other tattoo, about the name on her ankle, and if that was the first time Mum had talked about me. If he was surprised she had a daughter my age. If he'd asked about Dad. If he'd stopped asking when he saw how her expression changed.

Outside, it had stopped raining. There was no trace of Corpus Cristi now; we'd entered a different city where it was hard to believe Corpus Cristi could exist at all. As though it was a dream. Or maybe the dream was where we were now, and I'd get up on Tuesday and not remember a thing.

Brick high-rise buildings loomed on both sides, with huge glass entrances through which you could see porters all wearing identical uniforms. People walked under the tall trees lining the pavements with their umbrellas still open, too focused on avoiding the puddles to realize it had stopped raining. At the traffic light, beside an enormous glass building where there were three or four offices with the lights on, a man came to the car window to beg for spare change. The driver shook his head and when the man went on to the next car, for a second I thought he looked like Dad. Then the man driving the SUV next to us, which inched forwards as soon as the beggar approached, started to look like Dad too. Neither of them actually was, but if they had been it wouldn't have mattered. The car moved off again.

The closer we got to the mountains, the more the streets twisted and turned, as though to avoid inconveniencing the buildings and the people who lived in them. The streets meandered like rivers, practically empty, and most of the cars we saw were parked. It felt like they weren't real streets, like we were in some kind of theme park. And we kept climbing and climbing, till you could see practically the whole city in the spaces between the buildings. That view made it easy to feel like the city was yours, all of it, like it was only there to be looked at, at night and from above, after a rainstorm. I looked for La Alborada, wanting to see Aunt Anahí's building, but I couldn't find it. What was she doing? Changing the bucket under the leak? Watching a film about herpetologists? Smoking a cigarette in the kitchen? I would have liked her to be waiting for us in the hallway of Jorge's building, to have someone I knew at the party, someone who really knew me. The car started to slow down.

'We're here,' Mum announced, smiling.

Only when I opened the door did I realize my hands were sweating.

The building was new, or looked new. A high-rise. Must have been twenty storeys. Several balconies looked out onto the street behind glass railings, bearing plant pots, tables, a lonely BBQ or two, wet with rain. To get to the entrance you had to go down a little ramp that looked like it was made of marble, with a still pool on either side of it. I liked the way the lights reflected in the water. I imagined that, if we ever brought Katya, she'd fling herself at the water for a drink, almost throttling herself on the lead as I struggled to hold her back. I liked the idea. I'd like it if Jorge invited us to celebrate Mum's birthday or Christmas there, and even let us bring Katya.

I saw myself again in the glass door and adjusted my top a bit. I smiled. *You're going to like me, Jorge, so much that you're going to invite us over for Christmas.*

The porter stood up from his post. Mum greeted him and he came to open the door. I was surprised that he not only recognized Mum, but that they knew each other's names.

'The lift's on its way down, Señora Milena.'

'Thank you, Don Félix.'

I smiled and said hello quietly before following Mum into the building, as though worried that if I lagged too far behind I'd be left outside. How many times had Mum been here? Enough for the porter to know her name. To get to the lifts we crossed a little waiting room, a black leather sofa set next to a staircase so wide three people could climb it next to each other. At the back of the building were three lifts with silver doors, each one with a little black screen showing red numbers.

Without us needing to press a button, one set of doors opened with a little ding. The lift had enormous windows looking out over the entire city. Mum paid no attention to the view, using the window as a mirror so she could sort her hair out at the back, where it had got squashed against the car headrest. The doors closed.

'Which floor?' I asked.

'They've already called it,' she replied, still combing her hair with her fingers. 'It opens right into the flat.'

'Fancy.'

For a second, I imagined Aunt Anahí fixing her hair in the glass, with the same gestures as Mum, before turning to me to ask if she looked OK. And I imagined telling her she did, that she had nothing to worry about, that Jorge was really lovely and she was going to like him. A little ding announced seconds in advance that the lift was about to move. I started picking at my little finger, looking for a cuticle to yank.

'Meli…'

Mum turned to look at me but didn't say anything. Meanwhile, the numbers changed, 2, 3, 4. I smiled as though to say she had nothing to worry about.

'How long has it been since you saw each other?' I asked.

5, 6, 7.

'Like, two weeks.'

Two weeks? I yanked at my cuticle. We hadn't seen each other for seven months. I stopped smiling.

Had she come to the city without telling me?

8, 9, 10.

Before I could ask whether Jorge had been to Bucaramanga or she'd come to Bogotá, she spoke.

'Meli, I haven't told him.'

'Told him what?'

11.

'That you're my daughter.'

There was another little ding, and the doors opened.

After locking the bathroom door, I ran my hands over my abdomen. I was coming apart, I could feel the stitches falling out one by one, giving way to a black hole that was growing and growing. It wasn't the first time I'd come apart. When I broke my thumb – when I heard it break – I tore right open, as though all the stiches that had been holding me together had been ripped open with a scalpel. My stomach dropped to my feet and my brain shot out upwards and was on the brink of disappearing, like the bubbles in Coke, and in the middle, in the vacuum that my stomach and brain had left, I began sinking, disappearing, deafened by a shrill ringing. It wasn't pain. It was something much worse.

There was a red flower in a pot in Jorge's bathroom. It was the guest bathroom, small, no shower. I tried to take deep breaths. *In, out.* More than a hole, what I had inside was sort of like a tar pit, and the tar was dripping out of me faster and faster as I came apart one stitch at a time, like a rag doll, except instead of fluff what was pouring out of me was black tar. I grabbed a couple of the plant's leaves and yanked them off. Maybe if Mum had given me some warning that she had betrayed me, a couple of hours even, before the lift vomited us into the middle of Jorge's living room, it wouldn't have felt so awful. When Jorge greeted us, I was already coming apart.

He greeted Mum with a quick kiss on the lips. 'I'm so glad you're here, love,' he said. I was rooted to the ground, and would have been left inside the lift if Mum hadn't put a hand on my shoulder and given me a little push. I said nothing. 'You must be Melissa,' Jorge said. I thought, *Yes, I must be*. But I couldn't speak, I didn't know what I was allowed to say.

If Melissa wasn't Mum's daughter, then who was she? As though Mum had worked out the fix I was in, she said, her hand still on my shoulder: 'Yes, this is my little sister.' Bam! Another seam burst, the tar started spraying out. 'My little sister.'

Jorge said something, I don't know what, and smiled. He had a deep voice, perfect teeth, like something out of an advert, black curly hair, a slightly wrinkled forehead. He must have been about forty. We went into the living room, where several people were sitting, talking and laughing. In the middle was a little table bearing glasses of wine and a board of ham, cheese, and olives. I saw the people move their mouths and throw their heads back, but the sound of their laughter was delayed. Everything looked out of place. I didn't understand how these people could smile and chat and put a piece of cheese in their mouth as though everything was fine. But no, things weren't out of place, everything was in its place, except for me. It was me that didn't fit, not ever.

I shouldn't have told Mum about the fight.

That was it. Mum had realized, as I had, that nothing had changed. I sat on the sofa beside her, still prepared to try and find the right combination of words that would please her. I thought there must still be some way of showing her she could tell Jorge the truth, there must be something

I could do so that she'd want to tell him the truth, even if she did it later, when all these people had left. That's why I tried to pay attention, to smile, to reply to Jorge's questions, as though black bile wasn't dripping out of my chest. He asked me about school, about basketball, about my aunt, and I realized Mum had talked to him about me. But far from liking that, it made my stomach churn even more, as something became clear to me that maybe should have been obvious from the beginning: it was an old lie.

You must be Melissa.

It wasn't the fight that had convinced Mum. She'd made the decision before I told her I hadn't fallen over, before picking me up to go to Corpus Cristi, before calling me, long before. Since the first time Jorge found my name tattooed on her ankle? And if it wasn't for that, would she have even told him about me at all?

To deny someone is to betray them, Zapata would have said. And what if the opposite of love isn't hate, but shame? Peter was worse than Judas, Zapata would have said. Hate is selling your neighbour for a few pieces of silver or a flat with a view, whatever, it makes no difference to the person being sold. Sitting in the living room, I stopped following the conversation, which had moved on to something or other that Jorge's friends found entertaining. A waiter, dressed all in white except for a black bow tie, passed me a glass of wine. I brought it to my lips and downed it in a few long gulps. Mum looked at me as though asking me to take it easy. No fucking way. I put the empty glass down on the table. I felt like interrupting the conversation to say, 'Right, so are you telling him, or am I?' But that wasn't what I wanted, I wanted her to *want* to tell him, I wanted not to have to think about it, to be able to eat the cheese and ham in peace, tell a funny anecdote, say how lovely the view from the flat was, call her 'Mum'.

I got up and asked where the bathroom was. As I walked across the living room, I felt like I was leaving a trail of tar that would seep into the wood. I locked the door and turned on the tap to splash a bit of water on my face. *Breathe.* Mum had had two days to warn me. I yanked another leaf off the plant, ripped it in two, three, four, until there was no leaf left and the bits were all over the floor. I yanked off another. *But it would be stupid.* And another. Incredibly stupid, to believe that Mum would come back for me. To believe we'd see each other more often, believe I had changed, that she had changed. My fingers were green and I'd run out of leaves, so I ripped off the flower. *What an idiot, idiot, idiot.* The crushed flower made the exposed flesh where I'd ripped off my cuticle sting. I yanked the petals off harder. My skin was red with blood, mine and the flower's.

Someone knocked on the door.

'Engaged!'

'Meli?'

I let the bits of petal fall to the tiles and clenched my fists. I didn't answer.

'Are you all right, love?'

'Why didn't you tell him?'

She was silent for a while and then she answered.

'He wouldn't understand.'

Understand what? What the fuck does that mean, Mum?

I don't know when I'd started beating the wall with my knuckles, but they were tingling, stinging, on fire, really, because they were already swollen from that morning. I wanted them to hurt more.

'Leave me alone.'

The body can only feel one kind of pain at a time, they say. *Maybe when all the skin and all the muscle falls off and only the bones are left, maybe then it'll be my hand that hurts.*

'Meli…'

'I've got a nosebleed.'

'Do you want me to…'

'No,' I interrupted. 'I just want to stay in here until it passes.'

'All right.'

I felt like punching the mirror until it smashed. Destroying the wall with my knuckles, destroying my knuckles with the wall. I kept punching, the tingling spreading down into my fingers.

What other lies had she told me? Was she really going to move back to Bogotá? If she did, she'd probably come and live with Jorge, in his enormous flat with a view of the entire city. She'd said she wanted me to live with her, but did she really mean it? Was she going to convince Jorge to let her little sister live with them? 'Poor thing,' she'd say, 'look, she's an orphan, the poor girl has no mum or dad.' She'd be right, I don't. Maybe if Jorge really loved her, he'd do it out of the kindness of his heart. Fuck that. *Fuck Jorge and his flat with a lift in the living room, fuck you, Mum, and your lies, and fuck me for having believed you.*

Someone knocked on the door.

'For fuck's sake, leave me alone!'

A voice I didn't recognize apologized on the other side. 'I didn't know there was someone in there.' My knuckles were bright red, they'd be purple tomorrow. I was coming completely apart, but I didn't care anymore about the tar spilling out of me. *Let it come, let it spill out, let it flood the bathroom, the flat, the city.* I wanted to break something. I wanted to run into the living room and pull Mum's neckline down to reveal that awful Tweety tattoo she hated so much, for everyone to see. 'Didn't expect that, did you, motherfuckers, that underneath all these pretty clothes there's this piece of shit,' I'd say. Then I'd scream that she was my Mum, you morons, can't you see how similar we are? You're really telling me, Mum, that you didn't think they'd figure out how similar we look? *What was it you said, Mum? The apple doesn't fall far from the tree? Not far at all.* It doesn't matter what clothes we wear, how much make-up we put on, underneath it all she's got her Tweety and I've got my bruise, it doesn't matter what we do, our mistakes are branded on our skin, forever, so we won't forget we're the same people as before, the same people we always were, because people don't change, they just lie.

Breathe, child, breathe.

Another knock at the door. 'Will you be long?' the stranger asked.

'Fuckssake!' I yanked the door open, wishing it opened outwards so I could slam it into the guy. He looked at me in confusion and I just walked out, but instead of going back into the living room I went down the corridor, further into the flat, looking for something I could kick until it broke. I felt like the tar wasn't something coming out of my chest, out of me, it wasn't something that could come out of me, it *was* me. I was that black bile, it was what I was made of, and that's how I saw myself, even though I had skin and was wearing clothes, I'd always been that way and now the disguise was falling off, one stitch at a time.

I found Jorge's bedroom. I went in and closed the door, meaning to destroy it. I didn't need to turn on the light, the light of the whole city came in through the huge window at the back of the room. I wanted to break it. I wanted to see the glass fly, for the noise of the city to come in, and the cold, the honking horns, the dirty air, all the shit, something real. I wanted to throw the chair in the corner out of the window, and then the desk, the bedside lamp and the TV, the pillows and the bedcovers, I wanted to empty the wardrobe and one by one throw out all Jorge's trousers, Jorge's shirts, Jorge's socks, Jorge's underwear, and watch them fall into the wet street. I imagined seeing them on the pavement, soaking in the puddles, covered in mud. Except no, that wasn't what I wanted, no, because then Mum would be right.

She'd see the furniture fall and splinter on the asphalt, she'd see the TV screen smash, the clothes fly, and she'd think, 'Look what she's done now, look what she did to Pilar Villareal, look what she did to the Martínez brothers' cat, look what she always does. Thank God I didn't tell Jorge the truth.' She'd say, 'Her? She's not mine, course not.' No, that wasn't what I wanted.

What I wanted was for her to come looking for me when I had an even bigger flat, much bigger, much nicer than Jorge's, when I was *somebody*, when I owned the city. For her to come to me for help, and for me not to let her in. When she was told she couldn't come in, she'd scream, 'But she's my daughter! That's my daughter!' and I'd look her in the eye and say, 'I don't know you.'

I opened the drawer in the bedside table to see whether Jorge had something to treat a headache in there. Inside, I found a watch. An enormous, heavy watch. His wrist must ache just from the effort of wearing it. *What an ugly watch, Jorge.* I held it up, yes, it was as heavy as it looked. *If I throw it against the window, it'll break.* It was practically new. *How could you leave a watch like this lying around, Jorge.* I was looking at the ridiculous little gold hands, the whole thing was ridiculous, its hands all swollen like a caricature of a watch. *And yet, think how much people pay to wear something this ugly.* How much people pay. I heard a whisper from another life: *I want to graduate, I want to graduate.*

I put it in my pocket.

Not top of the class, but I'll graduate.

I stood there for a moment. I waited. I don't know what I was waiting for. Someone to catch me, maybe, Jorge to come in suddenly, Mum to come looking for me, I don't know, but since nothing happened, I left the bedroom and walked straight down the corridor towards the lift. Mum saw me from the living room. I avoided her gaze and kept walking. I called the lift. Mum came up to me as I was waiting.

'Meli,' she said, before seeing that I'd already called the lift. 'You're leaving?'

'What does it look like?'

'Don't talk to me like that.'

The doors opened.

'See ya.'

I stepped inside, but she grabbed my wrist.

'Meli, wait, please.'

'Let me go.'

'Please, come on, let's talk.'

'I said, let me go.' I pushed her, hard, and she gave me a frightened look and made no further move to come closer. And, to make clear that this was the correct decision, I added: 'You know what I'm capable of.'

The doors closed with a little ding.

MONDAY, PUBLIC HOLIDAY

The dripping, that vacuum. The sadness that seemed to come from a future moment, from a pain not yet lived, had stopped being a drip. The crack had burst open, water had flooded my bedroom and was drowning me. The pain was no longer from the past or the future, it was here. It was now. I rolled over once more in my bed. At least I was home again. I squeezed my eyes shut. It was early. If I kept trying to get comfy, maybe I'd eventually find a position in which it would all disappear.

I gave it up as a bad job and sat up. I looked at my phone lying switched off on the table, saw myself reflected in the screen wearing last night's make-up, my black eye swollen, my hair tangled. I'd turned it off so I wouldn't have to hear Mum's calls, see Mum's messages, think about Mum at all. Was she worried about me or about what I'd done? Did she want to know if I'd got home OK or whether her little sister was a thief? *Why is she calling when she already knows?* I pushed my phone away so I didn't have to see myself reflected in it. *Everyone knows*. My bag was on the floor. I didn't want to see it, I didn't want to see what was inside, I wanted to pretend a while longer that it had all been a dream. *I know.*

I took a couple of steps across the room. I thought about going to the kitchen for a glass of water, but wanted to avoid Aunt Anahí. I was sure she must have heard me come in around midnight. I went back to bed and pulled the covers over my head, curled up into a ball so no part of me was exposed, but that vacuum didn't shift. I flung the covers off, got up and opened my bag. And there it was. None of it had been a dream. There it was.

What was I going to do with the watch? *Graduate.* But how? Who could I sell it to? I didn't even want to look at it. But what the hell, I'd come this far, better to sell it and do something useful with the money. And when people found out what had happened, they'd point at me and say: 'Look, she's been at it again, always the same with that one. She's a bad egg.' And I'd say, 'Yeah, so what?' They'd say, 'She'll always be a bad egg,' and they'd be right, but if I was going to be a bad egg, I may as well be an egg with a diploma.

Besides, what was the problem? Someone like Jorge could just go and buy himself another watch, he could go and buy himself the whole fucking shop if he wanted. *Poor little Jorge, he lost his ugliest watch.* I was never in my life going to own a watch like the one I was holding in my hands. *Fuck Jorge and his bad taste.* I repeated that over and over, and still, the vacuum.

The thing in my chest wouldn't budge. It wouldn't budge because it had nothing to do with Jorge's wrist, which had woken up without a watch, but with the hands that had taken it. Couldn't I be happy I'd found a solution and have done with it? I tried to imagine what it would be like to go in with the money the next morning, how it would feel to hold my diploma in my hands, to be in the photos, to hug Zapata. But the vacuum was still there.

I needed a shower. I knew I'd feel better after a hot shower, even if only for a little while. When I emerged from my room, Katya came over, wagging her tail. I wanted to tell her to save her excitement for someone who deserved it, but she wouldn't have understood, so I just stroked her head and scratched behind her ear the way she liked, before heading down the corridor.

A shower would make me feel better, I repeated, closing the bathroom door, but it would have to be a long one. While the water was heating up, I took off my clothes from the night before, my back to the mirror, and shook my head as I remembered how excited I'd been when I put them on. I wondered if Mum had called Aunt Anahí to tell her everything (unlikely) or whether any moment now I'd hear sirens and would look outside to find a police car outside the building (more likely).

I tried thinking about my restaurants. I imagined a huge garden, the kind with fountains and a hedge maze. There'd be a little house where all the cooking would happen, and the dishes would be quick things, sandwiches, pasta, crêpes, rice, things that could be made in advance and kept in a picnic basket. People wouldn't know exactly what was in each basket, all they'd have were a few words like 'romantic' or 'hen party' or maybe something abstract like 'blue', 'daughter' or 'thief'.

I sighed as the water ran over my forehead and nose and made my fingers sting, my face, my eyelid, my knuckles. I thought about my favourite idea, the restaurant that looked like a house where people would cook their own food, following the chef's instructions, and it suddenly seemed ridiculous. *Who would pay for something like that?* Incredibly rich people who had never cooked, people who didn't have Aunt Anahí.

She taught me to cook after Mum left. Back then my throat was a tight knot the entire time, and the slightest thing – a song, a phrase, a smell – was enough to make me miss her. And if I let myself miss her, the tears started falling, so to stop myself from crying I had to shout or break something. I would have done anything not to think about Mum. My aunt understood, it's why she didn't ask how I was or try to console me after she left.

One weekend, after Mum said she would visit but never showed up, I grabbed a pillow and tried to destroy it. I managed to rip the pillowcase and get some of the filling out, which I flung on the floor. Aunt Anahí, who'd been loitering outside, peered in only once I left the pillow alone. She told me to come into the kitchen and help her with lunch and then left, without waiting for me. Maybe that's why I followed her, or maybe I just didn't want to be alone. Once I was in the kitchen, she told me to start chopping garlic, and pulled out a plastic bag. I grabbed a knife and got going on the garlic bulb, which was whole and unpeeled.

'Christ alive! No, no.' She stopped me. 'Not like that, child.'

She showed me how to peel it, then pulled out a clove and demonstrated how to slice it. I ended up with these huge bits, all different shapes; as I sliced, some rolled onto the floor, where Katya sniffed at but didn't eat them. Anahí didn't say anything about how bad a job I'd done. Instead, she told me to put them in the plastic bag. Then she added a chicken breast, some lemon juice, a bit of oil, cumin, some Colorey, salt and pepper, and sealed it tightly.

'And that's how you make chicken adobo,' she said, before putting the bag on the countertop. 'Now punch it.'

'What?'

'Like this,' she replied, and she started giving it little jabs with her fist. 'Start on one side, then the other, the whole thing.'

She moved away to check on the pot of rice and I copied her. I punched the chicken a couple of times, harder and harder, until I was thumping loudly on the countertop.

'Right, I think it's dead, kid,' she said, laughing. 'Now, leave it alone and come and watch how to make the rice.'

I ended up smiling too.

When I got out of the shower, I realized I didn't want to be by myself. Anything was better than being alone with that vacuum unstitching my skin from my neck to my belly button, leaving the black tar pit exposed.

There was noise coming from the kitchen. I went in carefully, almost on tiptoes. Aunt Anahí was in front of the stove melting a lump of butter in a pan. Katya ran to greet me, lifting her paws up onto my chest as I crouched down to stroke her.

'You hungry?' asked Aunt Anahí, swivelling the pan to dissolve the butter.

There were two plates out on the side. I knew it didn't matter what I said, she was going to serve me breakfast. I smiled.

'Yeah.'

'Dice me some onion and tomato, then.'

I moved around the kitchen carefully so she wouldn't see my face. I got out a knife and started chopping the way she'd showed me. If you've got long onions, you have to take the green tops off so you're left with just the white part of the bulb. You slice vertically, following the lines on the onion. After a few cuts, the ends start opening outwards. If it splits into several chunks, repeat with each one and stack them together. Then you do really thin horizontal slices to give you little cubes that practically disappear in the pan. It's actually super easy. If you do it properly, it'll be done so fast you'll have finished the pile of cubes before your eyes even start watering, but if you do it badly and take too long, you'll have to wipe away the tears so you don't end up slicing a finger.

'I fucked up.'

Aunt Anahí came over and glanced at the onion on the chopping board before turning back to the stove.

'Looks fine to me.'

I put the knife down on the counter, my lip trembling.

'No… I shouldn't have gone with her this weekend.'

She went still, then left the pan on the stove and came back over to me.

'Kiddo, I… Bloody hell! What happened to you! Come, come here, stand under the light… My God, you look like Christ on the cross. What happened? Just look at you, who did this?'

'I did.'

She put her hands on my cheeks and I tried to move my face away because I didn't want her to look at me anymore.

'Oh, kiddo.'

'Don't.'

But instead of moving away, she hugged me fiercely. I stood motionless, not wanting her to hug me, but also not wanting to push her away. I felt her warm hands on my back and my chest started shuddering. She didn't say anything, she just hugged me. My throat felt tight, my face was getting hot, I had to get away or it was going to happen. I tried to move but she held on to me more tightly. That was what did it. My chest shook, my hands shook, and I felt the salty tears fall, disgusting as snot, and because I was so close to her I pressed my face into her shoulder as though to hide away, pretending the sobs shuddering through me were someone else's. They kept coming, the tears, the snot, the sobs, over and over, and there was nothing at all I could do about it.

Who knows how long I stood there, but by the time my breathing had calmed a little we could smell burning. My aunt let go of me to move the pan and turn off the stove. Then she held my hand and took me into the living room, where we sat down together on the sofa.

'Let it all out, little one,' she said, her hand on my back.

Let it all out, she said, as though I hadn't already soaked her shoulder.

She looked at me, and I wanted to tell her not to look at me like that, that I deserved my black eye more than I deserved that look, but when I tried to talk my lip trembled and suddenly I was telling her everything. The tears returned, my bad eyelid stung, my head hurt like I'd been drinking and the words came out in one endless sticky stream.

I told her everything. Everything. I told her what I'd done to Pilar Villareal, what had happened at Jorge's party, the watch, everything, repeating the same phrases over and over, without pausing, and I felt like the black tar was flowing out of me, yes, flowing out because maybe it wasn't me, but rather belonged to me, had belonged to me for a long time, but didn't need to actually be me. The bile flowed out, not through my chest now, but through my mouth, and spread itself around the living room and pooled on the carpet. And when I no longer had anything to tell, when I was empty, I covered my face with my hands to not have to look at the black bile everywhere, but especially so Aunt Anahí wouldn't have to see me.

'I'm a bad person,' I said, still hiding my face. 'There's something wrong with me, I don't know why I'm like this.'

I was silent, still shaking, hiding in the darkness of my hands. Now my aunt would see me for exactly what I was, a creature, yes, a creature who vomited toxic black bile, who had flooded the living room and perhaps even drowned her. Maybe that's why she was silent. But then she spoke.

'My first kiss,' she said, 'was from my friend Sebastián – Sebas – when we were fifteen. I liked him, I liked him a lot, that's why I got scared.'

I moved my hands away from my face to look at her, not knowing what to expect. She went on.

'Yep, I got scared and pushed him away and told him not to talk to me again, told him he was disgusting. And as if that wasn't enough, I blabbed to everyone else.' She sighed. 'And, well, I'm sure you can imagine. He ended up fighting with his parents, and the kids at school laid into him, and me, for good measure. I wish I could go back and do things differently, but I can't.'

She put a hand on my back.

'We never fully realize the hurt we can do to others, kid,' Aunt Anahí went on. 'But good people and bad people, that's just for telenovelas. What we do have, kid, are decisions. Good decision and bad decisions. The tough part is that there's always something to decide, yesterday, today, tomorrow. And those decisions are what make us who we are, in the end, don't you think?'

I think I understood. I don't know if I entirely believed her, but I understood what she was saying. Yesterday, today, tomorrow, simple words, but also so complicated. Decisions. Yes, decisions. Decisions yesterday, decisions today, decisions tomorrow. I took a deep breath. My chest was still shuddering and my head was pounding horribly but the tears had stopped. I lifted my hands from my face but didn't look at her, I just stared at the coffee table. Decisions today.

I remembered Margarita, the admin woman, and her question: 'So, what are you going to do?' I felt like she was asking me again, but this time it didn't paralyse me. I knew the answer.

'I don't think I'm going to graduate. Not now, at least.'

'Now, later, in a year, two, whenever,' Aunt Anahí said, putting her arm round my shoulders. 'I'll be there. You know why?'

'Because you've already bought a dress?'

'Exactly.'

I laid my head on her shoulder and allowed myself a little smile.

'I need to go to Jorge's.'

'Want a lift?'

'Thanks.'

'Breakfast first, though. Come on.'

She got up and held out her hand to me.

'But you're chopping the onions,' I said, before taking her hand. 'I've done enough crying already.'

'No, señora.' We headed to the kitchen. 'You'll be doing the chopping. And if necessary, you'll cry again, and talk again, to me, to your friends, whoever, but you'll talk.'

I followed her in silence.

'You are not a cork, Melissa Noriega,' she scolded me. 'You don't have to keep everything bottled up.'

I had the address saved on my phone. Still, part of me hoped I wouldn't be able to find the building and I'd have an excuse not to see Jorge's face. But there it was. Aunt Anahí parked in the street and I walked over to the porter. The building looked bigger in the daytime because of the way the light came in through the giant windows and reflected off the water. The porter opened the door for me, and when I told him who I was, I realized I didn't know Jorge's surname, so I just said, 'Floor 11,' to be clear. The porter rang up. I could still leave, I thought, turn round, get into the car and disappear.

'You can go on up, the lift's on its way.'

I would have preferred to take the stairs, at least that way I would be ringing the doorbell instead of appearing suddenly in Jorge's living room. But no, I had no idea where the stairs came out, and the lift was already on its way, so I waited and got in as soon as the doors opened. I felt a knot in my stomach that got bigger with every floor, but a knot was better than nothing, better than the vacuum I'd woken up with. I was sweating, too. I tried to rehearse what I was going to say, but I'd only managed two words before I arrived at the eleventh floor. The doors opened. Jorge.

He greeted me, friendly but uncomfortable, and then burst out: 'Are you all right?'

I realized he was looking at the bruises on my make-up-free face.

'I just wanted to return this.'

I pulled the watch out of my pocket and he took it with one hand as he held the lift door open with the other.

'I'm sorry,' I said.

'It was an accident,' he replied, trying to sound convincing. 'Could have happened to anyone.'

I gave him a crooked smile, to thank him for the white lie. The lift doors started to close, but he held them open.

'Are you sure you wouldn't like to come in? I think... maybe it would be a good idea for you to talk to Mile... she was quite upset yesterday.'

She was? *She* was quite upset yesterday? I thought again of how easy it would be to tell him the truth about us.

Three words, that was all I needed to drop the bomb. I still wanted to hurt Mum and if he gave me the opportunity, I would.

'I have to go,' I said, giving him a wave.

He let go of the lift door, thanked me, and as the doors closed, he said he hoped we'd see each other again. I didn't know if that was a good idea, us seeing each other again. Not Jorge, me and Mum. Probably not, not for a while, at least. She had hurt me, and I wasn't ready to tell her yet. Maybe one day we'd see each other and talk, like her and Aunt Magdalena on the beach. Yeah, maybe one day we'd walk along the shore together, two pairs of footprints in the sand, and maybe that day she'd believe me when I told her how much she'd hurt me.

There are conversations that are meant to be had beside the sea and others that are never meant to be had, that are meant to become black holes, but it's difficult to tell them apart. I looked at the city through the glass of the lift, as it descended one floor at a time. I thought of the song about the hill, about the first time Zapata had played it for me. I could almost hear it.

I'd left the dark house and run through fields with barbed wire and trees with leaves like curtains. I'd crossed rivers and got soaked up to my knees, I'd climbed the hill, not for minutes, but for whole days, a hill that looked small but from the top all I could see was the sky, a beautiful blue sky. And I'd made a deal and someone had swapped places with me and that was why, the only reason why I was now coming down the same hill, I had it under my control now, it was calm, at least for now.

I looked at my reflection and thought that the next day I'd wake up and feel a bit less awful, and the day after that I'd feel a bit better still, and so on until the day it was gone, only a memory, a bitter one, but a distant one too. *Wouldn't it be nice*, I thought as the lift doors opened, *to be able to talk to that Melissa, the one for whom these things are a distant memory*.

How nice it would be if the two of us could walk along the beach – just for an hour, that's all I ask – and be able to ask that future Melissa what was going to happen. Ask her if we graduated, if we had a restaurant, or several, one with Zapata, if Karen was happy, if Víctor had expanded the garage, if Aunt Anahí had found love, if we were talking to Mum, if all the rage, the hate, the tar had disappeared (or if there was a bit less of it, at least), if we were happy. The other Melissa wouldn't even have to tell me everything, maybe she wouldn't even have to speak, it would be enough for her to hold my hand as though to say, 'We're going to be OK,' and I'd believe her.

I said goodbye to the porter and as I left the sun hit me full in the face. I walked over to the car, where Aunt Anahí was waiting.

If I could meet the old Melissa, I'd tell her not to buy the avocado coin purse because we'd never used a coin purse and definitely weren't going to start now. I'd tell her how to de-vein prawns and how to make chicken adobo, I'd tell her you can't trust cats, not even to stay alive, and that she shouldn't be afraid of losing Uncle Roberto. That she should give Zapata a hug when she finds her smoking in the bathroom and another to Víctor when he comes looking for her before school because his dad's in the hospital, that you have to tuck your thumb in properly when you punch something because otherwise it'll break, to give Karen a big hug and Dayana too, because an important part of us will stay with them forever.

I'd tell her that, fine, nobody likes mewling, nobody likes crying, but sometimes that's how you get rid of the black bile; that it doesn't matter what you do, what you say, what you wear, if Dad decides to leave, he'll leave, and if Mum decides not to come back, she won't come back, and that won't always be a bad thing, though it will always hurt. I'd tell her all that, but she might not listen to me, she might not believe me, actually, there's no way she'd believe me, so maybe it would be better not to say anything and just take her hand as though to say, 'We're going to be all right.'

'Let's get out of here, kid!' Aunt Anahí called from the car.

I smiled and opened the door.

'I'm still going to graduate,' I said, as I got in. 'I don't know when, but I'm going to. And do you know what I'd like that day?'

'To go dancing?' she asked, starting the car.

'Obviously, but also, when you show up in your new dress and I say to everyone, hey, this is my aunt, I'd like for someone to say that I look like you.'

Aunt Anahí smiled. The car started moving.

'Yes. I'd like that too.'

STEVNS TRANSLATION PRIZE

Peirene Press | Two Lines Press

The Stevns Translation Prize, run by Peirene Press (UK) and Two Lines Press (US), was launched in 2018 to support emerging literary translators.

Open to all translators who have not yet translated a full-length work of fiction, this annual award rewards great translation and creates new pathways into the profession.

The winner receives a commission to translate a text selected by Peirene Press and Two Lines Press, a six-week retreat in the French Pyrenees, including travel costs, and a dedicated, one-on-one mentorship throughout the translation process.

The Stevns Translation Prize opens for submissions in October and focuses on a different language every year.

With thanks to Martha Stevns, without whom this prize would not be possible.

THE PEIRENE SUBSCRIPTION

Since 2011, Peirene Press has run a subscription service which has brought a world of translated literature to thousands of readers. We seek out great stories and original writing from across the globe, and work with the best translators to bring these books into English – before sending each one to our subscribers ahead of publication. All of our books are beautifully designed collectible paperback editions, printed in the UK using sustainable materials.

Join our reading community today and subscribe to receive three or six books a year, as well as invitations to events and launch parties and discounts on all our titles. We also offer a gift subscription, so you can share your literary discoveries with friends and family.

A one-year subscription costs £38 for three books, or £68 for six books. Postage costs apply.

www.peirenepress.com/subscribe

'The foreign literature specialist'

The Sunday Times

'A class act'

The Guardian